The ARTIFICIAL NEWFOUNDLANDER

The ARTIFICIAL NEWFOUNDLANDER

a novel

LARRY MATHEWS

BREAKWATER

Library and Archives Canada Cataloguing in Publication

Mathews, Lawrence, 1944-
      The artificial Newfoundlander : a novel / Larry Mathews.
ISBN 978-1-55081-323-4
      I. Title.
PS8576.A825A78 2010   C813'.54   C2010-900130-3

BREAKWATER BOOKS LTD. acknowledges the support of the Canada Council
for the Arts which last year invested $1.3 million in the arts in Newfoundland.
We acknowledge the financial support of the Government of Canada through
the Book Publishing Industry Development Program for our publishing
activities. We acknowledge the financial support of the Government of
Newfoundland and Labrador through the department of Tourism, Culture
and Recreation for our publishing activities.

Printed in Canada

  Canada Council Conseil des Arts
for the Arts du Canada

 Mixed Sources
Product group from well-managed
forests, controlled sources and
recycled wood or fiber
www.fsc.org Cert no. SW-COC-000952
© 1996 Forest Stewardship Council

for Claire

CHAPTER ONE

Okay. *In medias res.*

Home again, home again. Emily meets me in the front hall, something confrontational in her stance, an impression augmented by her dyed-blond hair, which is short and stands straight up, evoking images of spears or icy stalagmites. At moments of intensity her eyes' blueness seems stronger than usual; the rest of her face seems to disappear, all her psychic energy beaming full blast at the enemy. Which can't possibly be her father, can it?

"Foley is coming," she says. "Has come."

I stand there, wishing there were some decorous way to push her aside so I can get to my bedroom to change into my running clothes. At the same time I'm wondering how many wives refer to their husbands by their surnames.

From the living room I hear the teenage Bosnian babysitter, hired last week so that Emily could begin her job search, reading to Samantha:

"Little Boy Blue, come blow your hurn / The sheep's in the meed-oh, the cow's in the curn."

"Coming here," I say, playing for time.

"Not here, to this house. Over my dead body. Here, St. John's. He's followed me. He wants to start over, he says. By which he means going back to Vancouver with him. It's not going to happen."

She stops. Though my daughter's been here for about three weeks, she's never told me exactly why she left Foley. I've assumed infidelity, the default reason. Can't beat the old standards. And why would that be unforgivable?

"Where is the bo-ee who looks after the sheep?" The babysitter, Sunila, must have paused for a moment to tune into the domestic drama. She's dark, small-breasted, large-bottomed. Soon she'll be moving with her family to Alberta, where her parents, unemployed since they arrived as refugees, will find work in the meat-packing plants.

"And what do you think should happen?" I ask Emily.

She huffs impatiently. Evidently the answer is so obvious as to be not worth expressing.

"Under the haystack, fast asleep."

"I want you to promise that you won't let him set foot in this house."

The subtext here is that Foley was my student – and sometime drinking buddy – before he became her lover, and that in the past he's tried to trade on some putative intimacy between us. Is it possible that she doesn't trust me to be 100 % onside? If this is a test, I'd better pass it, quick.

"I promise."

She moves enough for me to squeeze past.

"Weel you wake him? No, not I."

I visit my study to divest myself of the standard-issue prof's briefcase that I've hauled back from the university, where I've been internal examiner at a Ph.D. oral, one of the few formal job-related requirements of this, my "research" semester. Not the most pleasant way to spend a hot July afternoon, especially given a topic like "Postmodernism, Posthistory, Apocalyptic Conspiracy: A Study of Six Recent American Novels." Ms. (now Dr.) Thorne argued that if we deafen ourselves to the trendy bells and whistles, we can hear that whiny creaking noise of the venerable lefty artistic assembly line whose purpose is to turn out ever-newer-model critiques of capitalist injustice. A thesis eminently acceptable, the standard combination of sophistication and tunnel-visioned gullibility that passes for intellectual achievement, the whole enterprise surrounded by an aura of not-really-mattering.

"Nobody believes in ideas anymore," a senior colleague bellowed at me several years ago. "It's like Club Med. You've got tokens instead of real money."

9/11 happened last year, but as the supervisor, Dr. Eddie Laskowski, explained, since the research and most of the writing had been done before then, it would be unfair to insist that the dissertation be revised to reflect the fact that the term "posthistory" has become problematic. History, he acknowledged ruefully, is probably not quite over yet.

Off to the master bedroom, where I've had no company for some months now, a fact that doesn't trouble me as much as one would expect. My last liaison, if that's not too dignified a term, ended in February under circumstances too banal to rehearse here. The marriage that produced Emily has been dead for about a decade now, Sandra – the ex – now living in Ottawa. Well. Maybe, at fifty-eight, it's time to pack it in, though my body says otherwise. "Stay tuned," it says. "I'm not going to let this go on forever." Good luck to it.

Off with the prof costume, on with the shorts, the tee-shirt, the white socks. Time to blow this popsicle stand. Sunila will be off-duty soon, and Emily will therefore soon be scolding Samantha, who's not quite three. Emily seems freshly horrified each time Samantha disobeys her, as though being admonished for throwing a spoon ten minutes ago should now result in the exercise of restraint as she stands on tiptoe to grab some forbidden object from the kitchen counter. My other grandchild, Ryan, seven, insulates himself from Emily's wrath by parking his butt in front of the computer, solemnly exploring the world of, for example, dinosaurs as mediated by Ms. Frizzle and the fun-loving but sensibly docile kids of *The Magic Schoolbus*.

Out the front door, I pause for a moment and turn to the right to check out the grey knob of Cabot Tower emerging from the rock of Signal Hill. I do this every once in a while for no particular reason. After eighteen years here, I'm still a tourist in certain superficial ways. Lifelong denizens of the place wouldn't notice. I myself had to point the Tower out to the real estate guy who sold us the house. He blinked uncomprehendingly and didn't respond; southern exposure in the backyard was his big external selling point, Tower-gazing clearly an aberration appropriate only to mainlanders.

When I first came to the city, for my job interview, the then-head of department met me at the airport and whisked me to the top of Signal Hill in his four-wheel drive. "Whaddya think? Whaddya think?" barked Dr. Fabian O'Callahan, who liked to cut to the heart of the matter and did not suffer fools gladly, qualities that led to his being the victim of a *coup d'état* a couple of years later. I looked out at the grey ocean on one side, having already viewed the grey harbour on the other. There were tired-looking patches of snow on the slopes. It was mid-April, overcast and windy. What was he expecting me to say?

"It's, um, quite impressive."

O'Callahan nodded briskly, perhaps having decided already to write me off as an idiot, not that that would disqualify me for a tenure-track position. I had no sense of what the locals wanted or expected from me – and for that matter, if by accident I gave it to them, would they think the less of me for that? (Another mainlander reacting precisely as predicted.) Learning to live here has in part been a matter of coming to understand the irrelevance of such questions.

Driving to Quidi Vidi Lake, site of my run, I glide along the street whose name changes three times in less than a kilometre, peripherally aware of the harbour and the Narrows downhill to the right and of the major land-marks to the left – the constabulary's fortress, set well back from the street, the new art gallery/museum/ whatever rising unobtrusively behind a screen of trees, and then, after the curve to the right where Harvey Road morphs into Military, the Basilica.

Emily continues to preoccupy me. Her original plan seemed innocuous enough: she would bring the kids east this summer to visit both maternal grandparents. After a week in Ottawa at Sandra's, they showed up here. On the second day, after a few tentative comments about how absurd it is for me to be "rattling around" by myself in so large a house, she announced – the proper word, preceded by throat-clearing and body language conveying a sense of the imminence of the oracular – that she was leaving Terry Foley. That she intended, if possible, to stay here for the foreseeable future. That the future could be perceived to extend at least as far as Ryan's enrolment in grade two at Bishop Feild. That by "here" she meant St. John's, not necessarily this particular house. In fact she could leave at very short notice, find a cheap place downtown somewhere, if it was really important to me to have the house – "a house of this size" – all to myself. She had, she reminded me, been working more or less full-time for several years now and had a few dollars saved. And splitting from Foley would be beneficial financially as well, given that Foley's fellowship money had pretty much run out. So she had no intention of being a burden on me.

Home, according to the Frost poem, is where, when you go there, they have to take you in. Or alternately, as another character in the same poem says, it's something you haven't to deserve. The Republican and Democratic ways of looking at it, Frost said once. This flashed through my mind – I remember studying "The Death of the Hired Man" in grade eleven or twelve, *circa* 1960 – as Emily was speaking. I was hoping to come up with some witty Canadian spin, some way of informing her, in a lightheartedly ironic manner, that she was welcome, would always be welcome, meaning that I love her and therefore her children in ways that neither of us would care to articulate even if we could. (Why not?) But no phrase came, and after a moment's silence – which no doubt Emily, aficionado of the worst-case scenario, interpreted as my careful consideration of the possibility of giving her the boot – I said, "No problem. You can stay." And then, thinking that wasn't strong enough, "Of *course* you can stay."

There's a subtext here, one that springs from the early time, post-Sandra, when Emily unexpectedly asked if she could stay with me, and my short answer, reluctantly delivered, was a regretful No.

Back in the present, I'm through the ridiculously complicated intersection at Rawlins Cross and past the Colonial Building (will it ever be post-?). I turn left onto Bannerman, go past the playground, swimming pool, and ball diamond, turn right onto Circular Road. A move which never fails to bring to mind my "research interest," the unread novelist Father Alphonsus Ignatius Cleary, OMI (Oblates of Mary Immaculate), who described the residents of this end of Circular as members of the old-money old-blood old-bullshit gang, smugly ensconced behind their Wizard-of-Oz facades of worldly ostentation and pompous rhetoric. Or words to that effect, to be found in *Sacrament of Ashes*, his autobiographical first novel.

Cleary – priest, novelist, academic – was that rarest of species, a Newfoundlander who loathed Newfoundland and chose to live elsewhere, not an obvious choice either. Of course no one here has ever heard of him. Almost no one anywhere else, too. That his work has been universally ignored makes him an ideal research subject for someone who can do without intense academic competition. Translation: since no one else is interested in publishing on him, I don't have to bust my ass to ride the non-existent crest of the imaginary wave.

And the man himself? Presumed dead. Disappeared in 1985 under suspicious circumstances, body never found, not, apparently, that anyone was all that keen to find it. The vanishing act got a certain amount of press in Ottawa, where he was living at the time, but nary a ripple in the media here. What little I know about Cleary's life comes mostly from a brief correspondence with his publisher, Tom Wetmore, who used to run something called Muskrat Tale Press, until various government funding agencies grew tired of his incessant whining. Wetmore lived in Ottawa, too, and had a number of face-to-face meetings with Cleary but claimed not to know him well. He published all four of Cleary's novels, in print-runs of 500. Since there was no budget for marketing, they all quickly disappeared without a trace, a fate typical of most of Wetmore's productions.

I've found two reviews of *Sacrament of Ashes*. One complains that the dedication – "To the Fourth Member of the Quaternity" – is blasphemous. The other objects to the fact that the epigraph, from the "Ode to Joy," is not translated from the German.

Which fondly remembered thought motivates me to start to hum the last movement of the Ninth, drowning out the patronizing university horticulturalist on the CBC gardening call-in show. ("No, my love, there's nothing you can do about dandelions.")

One last tricky intersection and it's gently downhill past the grandly named but now doomed Stadium – former home of the St. John's Maple Leafs, now waiting for city council permission to become a supermarket – and down to the lake itself where I park in the shade of a tree on the other side of the chain-link fence separating the Anglican cemetery from the land of the living.

I approach the trashcan that is my invariable start and finish point. Roughly two and a half miles around the lake. If I can do it in twenty-three minutes, I'm ecstatic. Counter-clockwise is my preferred direction, manic fixation on the task at hand my *m. o.* Yes, one registers, briefly, the prison walls on the right, the boathouse past them on the left, incarceration and pleasure proffered like clichéd images of wise and foolish "lifestyle choices," reminding me for a moment – state-specific memory, no doubt – of the scene in *The Loneliness of the Long-Distance Runner* when the kid (Tom Courtney?) is allowed out of the juvenile detention centre early in the morning to go on training runs through the nearby fields and woods. We look down on him, so we don't miss the contrast between the squat building and the pastoral realm he belongs in.

My world is cut up into fifteen-second chunks: can I make it to that tree on the left, that bench on the right? If I meet someone I know, it's annoying. I want this space to be private, only strangers tolerated, and they'd better not be blocking my flight path. Poignant minor distraction: breasts gently bouncing in sports bras, gone in the twinkling of an eye, before proper appreciation can set in.

Coming around the far end of the lake, where the boardwalk meets the road that goes into Quidi Vidi village, I think of the one exception to my policy of unsociability, a gentleman of colour, perhaps a decade older than I am; for several consecutive years I would regularly meet him coming toward me, walking purposefully. It got so we would exchange monosyllabic greetings maybe three times a week. He was tall, slim, bespectacled, wore an old guy's grey cap. Once, as I was struggling against the wind near the entrance to the military base, he said, "Keep it up, man. You doin fine." It was the longest speech ever to pass between us. I couldn't discern an accent. Who is this guy? What's his story? He hasn't shown up in two years now. I miss him every time I run.

I make it back to my trashcan in 23.15, a sad performance in the larger context of personal bests, last year's times, and so forth, but the best I can do today. "All you can do," as they say here, which means, approximately, "Have the humility not to judge yourself over-harshly in this world of stacked decks and loaded dice."

I walk beside the cemetery fence for a minute or two. In the strong sun the headstones look soiled and fragile. St. John's, city of cemeteries. City of dreadful night. Well, not exactly. Nonetheless I believe it's salutary to have reminders of mortality made so blatantly public. Concentrates the mind, or should.

On the way home it's Terry Foley, not Alphonsus Cleary, who occupies my mind. If Cleary is a sort of Platonic ideal of the Newfoundlander, that is, an object of contemplation I'll never have to deal with in the flesh, then Foley is the living, breathing Newfoundlander with whom I have had, willy-nilly, most to do. My prodigal son-in-law, arriving so soon after my daughter, like the lethal right cross that follows the left hook.

The combination of Emily and Foley has always been an enigma to me. Perhaps it's always this way with fathers, but this case, objectively viewed, would surely vex any observer. Foley, working-class Corner Brook Catholic, comes to St. John's, falls under the sway of a genially charismatic Marxist history prof, and an intellectual is born – never mind that the expiry date stamped on his forehead has already passed. And it's not so simple. For – and here's where Emily came in – Foley was also infected by the bizarre strain of Anglophilia that, despite everything, survives in vestigial form in Newfoundland. Emily displayed just enough trace elements of Sandra to tip the balance in her favour.

Need it be added that the history prof, Fred Cragg, is a working-class Brit who specializes in the working-class history of the Bolton region, the very working-class place from which he, coincidentally, hails. He's reputed to have considered running as a Communist in the last provincial election but decided not to on the grounds that he didn't want to take votes from the NDP, a number estimated by others to be somewhere between eight and twelve. I would have given him mine, though, *épater les bourgeois*, as though such a thing were possible here.

Foley's own championing of the underdog, however, would not be about to stop with the white working class. For the last four years he's been in Vancouver working on his dissertation in Middle Eastern history, his thesis having to do with the sociological implications of sewage systems in various communities in nineteenth-century Syria – a project hindered, Emily has cattily informed me, by his inability to get through a required course in introductory Arabic. But he does have a predictable take on who's getting shafted in the region today. Hint: it's not the Israelis.

I could go on. He's been heard to call cab drivers "old boy," unaware that he's being condescending. He calls the bathroom "the loo." He's meticulous about referring to newspapers as "tabloids" or "broadsheets." He picked up this sort of thing in five years in St. John's.

What did Emily see in him? In the early days she would speak of him affectionately, but even then with a certain edge, as though she had judged him to be, despite appearances, eminently civilizable, and damn it, she would see the mission through to its conclusion. But that sort of rhetoric disappeared some time ago.

As I pull into the driveway, I find myself, perversely perhaps, looking forward to seeing Foley again. His companionship was important to me at one difficult juncture in my life, however multitudinous his short-comings. And it'll be interesting to hear what account he'll give of his current marital situation: one that will no doubt feature genuine bafflement at Emily's actions coupled with a desire to attach an appropriate degree of blame to himself, if only he could figure out why he deserves it.

I get out of the car, still sweat-soaked from the run, anticipating my shower. And then, as I close the door, I stop.

There's a moment like this in almost every day. I

hold up my right hand and stare from close range. I'm fascinated.

There should be a twelve-step program for people like me. "My name is Hugh and my life has, I'm sure, been warped in various unknown and probably insignificant ways by the fact that I have a minor deformity."

"Hi, Hugh."

It's the pinky finger, which is somehow (a) only about half there in terms of width – an inelegant but accurate way of putting it – and (b) fused or welded to its next-door neighbour. Perhaps it's been unsuccessful in its attempt to achieve fingerly freedom, gunned down in mid-jailbreak. Or possibly it's turned its metaphorical back on the world, and tried to burrow into its nearest sibling.

Either way, a source of meaningless quasi-embarrassment: for adults, worth a second or possibly third quick sneaky peek, and it's time to move on. Or is it? Perhaps the potential love of my life got an eyeful and turned away before we exchanged a word. Perhaps a man whose casual comment, rightly interpreted, might have changed my life, felt a shiver of revulsion at my handshake and cut things short with a nod. And it's always there and never a plus, its very existence an ironic challenge to my powers of interpretation. Original sin? My failure to become fully who I'm supposed to be?

And of course it explains my left-handedness.

Ryan has somehow understood that my hand is off-limits for discussion. Samantha, though, sometimes asks when it's going to be all better. I tell her that it might take a long time.

The moment passes. My appetite for contemplating my own ugliness – there is no other word – has been sated. I'm free to enter the house, that beacon of domestic normality, where I can play the role of benign patriarch regardless of physical appearance.

After supper I abandon Emily and the youngsters and drive up Signal Hill, in part a strategic retreat. I don't want to be too available to lend a hand during the interminable pre-bedtime activity, lest I be subject to permanent conscription. Not that overt commands or appeals would be issued, but Emily, like her mother, is a master at indirect hectoring, and will soon discover the parcel of moral high ground that comes with her new role as single mother.

I decide to sit in the car with my Tim Hortons coffee, imbibing the deceptively serene vista of endlessness that has over the years come to seem almost mundane. To look across at the lighthouse on Cape Spear, to be parked almost on the very spot at which Marconi proved that there was no stopping us from launching words across that endlessness: no big deal. Eighteen years in a place will do that to you.

I recall a scene from at least a decade back, a candidate for an Americanist job delivering his obligatory spiel to reluctantly assembled members of the department. A Melville man, he had no idea that the job was destined for a colleague's wife and that his quest for the Great White Tenure-Track Position was in vain. He talked about the early work, especially the depiction of

Americans who had traveled to the South Seas and stayed there. The exact content of his argument escapes me now, but I remember that he kept emphasizing that these characters were no longer really Americans, but neither, of course, could they be considered as authentically connected to the local culture. "They were neither one nor the other," he said. "They were hybrids, a strange mixture, belonging, in the end, to neither community."

I wonder what's happened to him, whether the early Melville has turned into a presentable meal ticket. I finish my coffee and begin to coast down homeward.

Much later, house quiet enough to allow the illusion that I have it to myself, I'm watching *Nightline*. The topic is astronomy, the latest discoveries. Colour pix of deep space. Lots of good lines. We all live in the Big Bang's afterglow, "a cold faint light," the reporter in the set-up piece says, "coming to us from all directions." There are objects in the universe older than the universe itself. Then there's dark matter, a ghostly background of particles we're not sensitive to. The universe is in the process of expanding forever, pulling everything apart.

In the kitchen to turn off the lights, I stop for a moment to look at one of the framed photos Terry Foley took of Ryan at five months, a strangely brooding poetic aura emanating from the fat little face.

CHAPTER TWO

"Merlin Kelliher, the improbably named protagonist of *Sacrament of Ashes* (1975), is clearly in many ways a fairly direct representation of Cleary himself."

I'm very unhappy with this sentence, but fixing it seems beyond my capacity at the moment. I'm working on the galley proofs for my 1500-word entry on Cleary for an encyclopaedia-like publication on Canadian literature due out in the fall. Of all such tomes, this will be almost the only one to acknowledge Cleary's existence, a gesture mainly due to the editor's desire to "give appropriate weight to regional writing." When I saw that line in an e-mailed blurb, I lobbied for Cleary's inclusion, receiving in response a form letter welcoming my contribution. Which makes me wonder how many other obscure "regionalists" have made the cut. Certainly there can be few as obscure as Cleary.

Isn't it redundant to say that anyone called "Merlin" is "improbably named," especially anyone born in St. John's around 1935? But do I want to leave the phrase in to make the point that I regard this choice of name as a bit silly, inspired as it obviously is by Cleary's decision to go for a bit of heavy-handed symbolism. Maybe I should leave it in.

And that's only the first problem. There's the awkwardness of "Cleary" echoing "clearly," which can be replaced by "obviously" – but that's not what I really want. "Obviously" would seem to imply some sort of incompetence on Cleary's part, when in fact he wanted the autobiographical connection to be blatantly available to careful readers. As though he had more than a dozen, poor bugger, the only publishing scholar of whom is yours truly.

"Merlin Kelliher, the protagonist of *Sacrament of Ashes* (1975), is in many ways a fairly direct representation of Cleary himself." Six minutes and thirty seconds have passed.

True, there are distractions this morning. The kid-related noise quotient from downstairs has increased, with the addition of a second caregiver, Sunila's friend Dobrila. At no extra cost, Emily has informed me: they'll simply split Sunila's modest wage. Dobrila is taller, leaner, sexier. And now the two chatter away at each other, language unidentifiable – they speak five, apparently – about God knows what. This will end shortly when Emily drives them all off to Bannerman Park for the rest of the morning, another annoyingly perfect one.

"Annoyingly" because I'm stuck inside with the proofs, which are supposed to be returned immediately, and because – the other source of distraction – this afternoon I'm to go *mano-a-mano* with Terry Foley, an encounter which promises no tangible benefit but seems oddly necessary.

Foley surfaced a couple of days ago. "I think a meeting would be helpful," he told me on the phone, his tone either solemn or mock-solemn, depending. Sometimes his ironic intent doesn't quite mask what's underneath it. "I would not be so churlish as to intrude myself on your hospitality unannounced. I know that would be ill-advised."

"Emily would shoot you," I shouted, my instincts from the old days kicking in. Uninterrupted, Foley would be unlikely to stop for a very long time. But now there was a brief silence.

"Has she acquired a firearm?"

"It's a figure of speech, Foley. Lighten up."

"Ah. Of course. You're right. Levity would be beneficial."

The dialogue meandered towards his main point, not a trivial one at that. As the father of Ryan and Samantha, he surely had some sort of moral – to say nothing of legal – right to have access to them. Perhaps, he suggested, that could be arranged through me. Then there was the issue of Emily's perceived irrationality in fleeing – his word – him and their life together. Perhaps I would be able to shed some light there.

"I was hoping you could fill me in on that one," I said.

"Oh. I see. Well, I have theories of course. Perhaps we could exchange intelligence."

Emily was not pleased to learn about the meeting. She senses the potential for major disloyalty on my part. The fact that I'm to meet Foley at the Ship has taken on a sinister symbolic significance for her, since Foley cherishes the notion that we were bosom drinking buddies before Emily came into his life.

"Just get this clear," she told me. "You're not going there as my representative. You are not authorized to make any commitment on my behalf."

That was yesterday. This morning she's meticulously distant.

"Merlin Kelliher, the protagonist of *Sacrament of Ashes* (1975), is in many ways a fairly direct representation of Cleary himself."

Do I need "in many ways" and "fairly"? What purpose do they serve other than to cover my ass in the extremely unlikely event that someone would attack me in print if they weren't there?

How many people are even going to glance at my Cleary entry, let alone look for ways to contest the banal and obvious points I'm making? The truth is that Merlin Kelliher *is* Phonse Cleary, or a dramatically enhanced version thereof. But you can't put things that baldly.

Then there's that charmingly anachronistic phrase "Cleary himself." Try getting that one past Eddie Laskowski, our department's ranking Theory geek.

But at this level these issues, mercifully, aren't relevant. The grad student proofreader will not give a flying fuck about the phrase "Cleary himself." I'm wasting time. Again. Another twelve minutes have passed.

I think I'm going to go with "Merlin Kelliher, the protagonist of *Sacrament of Ashes* (1975), is an imaginatively embellished version of Cleary himself." Apart from everything else, it's true.

I glance down the page. Extensive revision is out of

bounds at this point, but it's an okay job anyway, given the length limit: Merlin's youthful struggle to free himself from the baneful influence of his tyrannical father, a demonized version of Cleary's own; Merlin's love for his mother, a beatified, if not canonized, version of Cleary's own, the first of the idealized female figures who play major roles in three of his four novels; Merlin's escape from the spiritual deathtrap that was St. John's in the early fifties.

No space to mention the sly joke in the dedication: "To Elizabeth Anne Gulliford Cleary, 1913-1934." In fact, his mother died of a stroke in 1971; 1934 was the year his parents were married. I am perhaps the only living person in a position to make the connection.

I find this fact both exhilarating and pathetic. I'm in a fan club with one member. *The Loneliness of the Long-Distance Scholar.*

As for the Freudian implications of "Kelliher" – Kill-I-her – forget it. That sort of claptrap went out of fashion in the sixties, before which something as innocuous as Shakespeare's use of Syracuse in *The Comedy of Errors* could be publishably glossed as "Sire-accuser."

Come to think of it, the marriage of Cleary's parents would on the face of it make good Shakespearean comedy material. Elizabeth, only daughter of an irascible Presbyterian pillar of the merchant class, chooses James, lower middle-class Catholic, a person of no discernible distinction, then or now. The pillar disowns his daughter. The couple lives happily for a time.

But not ever after. Something darker takes over, and James devolves slowly into a domestic autocrat, a miniature version of Elizabeth's control-freak father. Cleary grows up in the midst of this emotional carnage.

As does Merlin Kelliher, in his parallel universe. Merlin, smartass autodidact, impressing the half-educated Christian Brothers who were his teachers, rebelling not by rejecting his father's religion but by declaring allegiance to a more rigorous and enlightened tradition within it and beyond it, his vicarious apprehension of mystical vision trumping the pettiness of rosaries, indulgences, denominational wrangling. Merlin worshipping his young mother, lamenting her wasted potential, her superiority to the world around her unrecognized. Merlin over-exuberantly – and silently – excoriating St. John's for its provincialism, its cultural and spiritual backwardness. No wonder that as far as I know, no one here has read Cleary, or heard of him, for that matter.

Still, I can see what Tom Wetmore saw in the manuscript that came sailing over his transom: a verbal energy indicative of a passionate spirit and strong, if largely negatively focused, intelligence. And there's a certain narrative drive, too, that gathers steam towards the end as Merlin decides to leave Newfoundland for-ever, his mother having died suddenly and conveniently. There's a final confrontation with his father, a symbolic dream sequence, and a brief epilogue in which Merlin leaves for England, never, we are given to understand, to return.

But Cleary, atypically enough for his time, left for Canada, not England, another of the many minor mysteries attending his life.

The morning is slip-sliding away. I promise myself

to look only for typos in the rest of the article.

The entrance to The Ship Inn is partway down the cement stairway connecting Duckworth and Water Streets, a fact that seems today to constitute a somewhat pretentious proclamation of its mythic dimension, its between-worlds status or some such nonsense. I approach from on high.

Foley is waiting for me. He rises, beaming. He's a big guy, six inches taller than me. I extend a hand, but he insists on a hug.

"Hugh," he says. "Me buddy."

"I'm your father-in-law, Foley. Let me go."

He complies, his point, he probably thinks, having been made.

It's mid-afternoon. We're alone except for the young barmaid, who's been watching us carefully. Her head has been shaved nearly bald, and she sports a pearl-coloured nose stud and an indecipherable shoulder tattoo, sad insignia of a generation struggling to distance itself from the rest of us. Good luck.

Perhaps Foley has already tried to hit on her; in fact it would be out of character for him not to have. To her, I'm probably a godsend, the cavalry arriving as the redskins are about to torch the wagon train.

"We're family," he says with a certain wry smugness clearly designed to amuse me. He turns to the barmaid. "This man is both my father-in-law and my best friend. Two pints of Smithwicks, my duck. He'll pay."

She mutters something noncommittal and gets to work.

In fact, it's hard not to be amused by Foley. There's something engaging about his pride in having been accepted as my equal. No longer prof and student, we're just two guys enjoying our shared guy-ness, though there is that slight complicating factor that he's the husband of my daughter, father of my grandchildren. But men of the world like us can take that in our stride; the important thing is the specialness that resonates between us as we drink. The thirty years that separate us are as nothing. Or so he seems to think.

"Cheers," he says, with the mock gravity that, in more congenial circumstances, is a touchstone of our fellowship. He still wears his hair unfashionably long. He still obsessively twirls the right end of his mustache between thumb and forefinger. The large colourless earring is new, however.

"So what's up with Emily?"

His brows knit and his face contorts, as though he were doing an impression of someone grappling with a novel metaphysical conundrum. "There are two major possibilities, I think. One is that it could have something to do with 9/11."

He pauses to gauge my response. We look at each other, both knowing that whatever the causes of Emily's behaviour, 9/11 would not make the shortlist. Why then is he saying this? He's long had me pegged as a small-l liberal of the sort who might under certain circumstances vote Conservative (true), has altogether too strong an affection for things American, including some of the wrong things (true), and – although the topic has never arisen between us – fails to perceive the obscenity inherent in the word "globalization" (true again). He no longer hopes to re-educate me, but believes it important that certain things be On The Record between us.

"Go on."

"Right. My analysis of 9/11 has always been problematic for her. Has she mentioned this?"

"No." In fact, I wouldn't swear that Emily is even aware of 9/11. The people I know tend not to speak of it, except implicitly in comments about the hassles of air travel. And even that's pretty much died out.

"Well. My first reaction was a sort of perverse satisfaction. Good for the hijackers, I thought. Of course later I reconsidered. It wasn't the CEOs who died in the Towers, it was mostly the peons. Like us."

He pauses, to make sure I'm okay with the idea of traveling with him in peonage class. Apparently the deaths of three thousand CEOs would have been regarded with total equanimity. My son-in-law, the moral cretin.

"Then of course I began to see the real horror, the Americans using it as an excuse to expand their hege-mony–"

"Yes yes yes. But Emily?"

"Couldn't get beyond the bourgeois thing about the deaths of individuals being all-important. Mostly white individuals, too, of course. I tried to interest her in the larger issues, develop a dialogue. Perhaps I became a bit wearisome on the subject."

"But 9/11 was almost a year ago. Why would she leave you now?"

"Might have been a cumulative thing. You know my tendency to pontificate." This is a standard rhetorical move for Foley – acknowledging the existence of something annoying about himself, employing a self-congratulatory tone as though he's actually done something about it. But he's looking confused, hurt. Maybe the phrase "leave you" is one he's been avoiding before now, a train pulling out of the station.

"No, she just said our life had become intolerable, and she didn't want to go into detail." He stares down at his glass.

"Cheer up, you'll always have me."

He smiles very briefly. "I must visit the loo."

While he's gone, I look around. Physically, nothing significant ever changes at the Ship. Perhaps it's for this reason that past Ship-selves so readily reanimate. I tune into a conversation I had with Sandra about fifteen years ago. It was the day Mario Lemieux scored the winning goal in the 1987 Canada Cup. Early evening in St. John's. What the hell were we doing there? Perhaps the prelude to an evening out, probably a play at the LSPU Hall just up the hill. We were at a table in the far corner, space today taken up by the low platform they've put in for musicians to perform on. The only other patrons, and there weren't many, were clustered around the TV on the other side of the room. A cheer went up, for Mario I later learned.

Sandra's blue eyes flicked toward the source of the noise. "Some silly hockey match," she informed me.

We would limp on together for another four years.

Foley returns. He contemplates his glass, wondering – I hypothesize – whether I'll be buying another round and therefore how quickly he can afford to drink what remains.

"You said there might be another reason Emily left."

He sighs, looks over his shoulder at the barmaid (reading a book), and lowers his voice. "There's a problem with my bird."

There's always a point in a Foley conversation at which I have to struggle to keep a straight face. "I see."

"Don't look like that. It can't possibly be sexual."

"It's about your bird, but it can't be sexual."

"An apparent paradox, I realize. I assure you that faithfulness has not been an issue."

"Foley, it's nothing to me one way or the other. I just want to find out why my daughter's unhappy."

"I wouldn't lie to you," Foley says, mildly offended. "And I'm not saying faithfulness has *never* been an issue. Two of a kind, aren't we? In any case. A couple of months back, I noticed certain … irregularities. You don't want detail, do you?"

"Detail is what I don't want."

"I sought conventional medical advice and received no joy. They claim not to be able to identify the source of the problem. I then consulted a practitioner of alternative medicine, who prescribed a regimen of expensive pills, with the proviso that I abstain from caffeine and alcohol." He gestures at his glass. "We both know how unrealistic that is. And so the difficulties persisted …." He lets his voice trail off, as though there is much more to be said, if only he weren't plagued by his damnable sense of decorum.

"And Emily …?" I cannot believe that I'm sitting here discussing what my daughter thinks about this man's penis. Perhaps this can be understood as a lesson in humility?

"'And Emily,' indeed. Has in one sense been understanding, in quotation marks. Doesn't seem to miss … anything. Has emphatically not been interested in … alternate approaches …." Again he stops. Even he would prefer not to cross this line.

"Yes. But would this be a motive–"

"Unclear. There was no dialogue on the subject. I'm speculating that, in the context of our entire relationship, this may have been some symbolic last straw."

"Still a dab hand with a cliché, I see."

He blinks, processes this unanticipated response, then smiles. "Ah, the old sense of humour is still functioning. But here's the irony. Since she left, I seem to be in some sort of … remission. I seem to be more or less back to normal."

"Foley the phoenix, bird miraculously reborn."

We clink glasses in deadpan celebration.

"I must go to the loo," I tell him.

The wall above the twin urinals in the Ship's washroom has undergone many changes over the years. For a long time, dating at least from the mid-eighties, its most noticeable feature was a cryptic equation in black magic marker: NFLD = Nigeria. What the hell did that mean? I'd wonder, every time I came in, though almost never before or after. Was it a reference to the civil war of the sixties – Ibos versus some other bunch I could never remember – with the implication that the symbolic equivalent might happen here? Catholics and Protestants? Baymen and townies? Newfoundlanders and come-from-aways? Any match-up I could imagine seemed absurd.

Or was it a more general statement about colonization? But if so, why Nigeria as opposed to any other victim of imperialism? It seemed clear that the inscriber must have had some specific point in mind, something whose precise resonance escaped me, a *parvenu* mainlander. Newfoundland as darkest North America, perhaps that was the wry point.

For a time I fancied that this equation might be the Rosetta Stone of the local psyche, which, if understood, would explain everything about the place. But no one, including me, ever mentioned it. By the time I'd returned to my table, I would have forgotten. Then at some point, in the early nineties perhaps, chalkboards appeared over the urinals and NFLD = Nigeria vanished forever.

Now the chalkboards have gone too. The repainted wall presents only a sparse, half-hearted sampling of current graffiti, as if male patrons of the Ship no longer aspire to wit or perhaps no longer carry writing implements on their person.

"Prostate trouble?" Foley inquires. This is not an attempt to insult or poke fun. It's a genuine stab at conviviality. If you're a geriatric and go to take a piss, you've probably got prostate trouble, in Foley's view of the world. Or maybe I've been in there longer than I thought.

When it's clear that I'm going to ignore the query, he asks for my take on the Emily situation.

"I really have come up empty so far. She's determined to stay here, but what's bothering her is a mystery. She hasn't exactly been forthcoming."

"I see."

This has depressed him even more. It occurs to me that he has actually expected me to have some sort of answer for him, that he still regards me as the guy who might have some accurate information about the world, though it's long been a joke between us that his real mentor is Fred Cragg.

Foley first showed up in my creative writing course around 1992, his head having for several years been stuffed with warmed-over Marxist goulash, the history department's perennial daily special. He wrote poems with titles like "Comprador," which to the best of my recollection started "You stand cursing / wallet crushing my windpipe / veins robbed / by the heartless razor you call / Profit." I encouraged a movement towards clearer syntax and more personal subject matter. He thought that this meant trying to write like Eliot, soon becoming adept at explaining how each line had four or five levels of meaning, only one of which was "the limited political sense."

At the beginning of the next semester, the course over, Foley showed up at my office with a bunch of new poems. Sandra and I were history at this point; I was often at loose ends, as they say. Foley and I started to meet every second week to discuss his work. At a certain point he let it be known that he had discovered Emily, and that this fact explained his new interest in writing "post-love poems," though it wasn't clear whether this phrase meant "poems written in the knowledge that conventional notions of love are obsolete" or "poems written after having sex." I didn't want to ask, either.

I remember feeling a mix of horror and jealousy about Emily. Horror for the obvious reasons: Foley had a department-wide reputation as a womanizer; details of his encounters (though not with Emily, of course) were

regularly proffered at our get-togethers, not with the
flamboyance of the callow bullshitter but rather as the
experienced tradesman talks about his craft. So Emily
would be hurt. But that wasn't all. How could she stoop
so low? He couldn't drive a car, couldn't be trusted not
to ask embarrassing personal questions of faculty
members at social gatherings, had never, as a child, been
read A. A. Milne. Different worlds, weren't they?

But there was jealousy too. Foley was *my* project,
after all, and I'd grown to like him, his eagerness to
learn, his ludicrous attempts to speak and act in ways
he deemed sophisticated, his need to be approved
of, metaphorically back-patted – perhaps, God knows,
echoing my own in that era of post-Sandra post-love.
And now my daughter had him, or he had her, or they
had each other.

The most striking image Foley authored that semester
was "the menstrual blood in the lovers' hourglass."
I remember reading it with some relief, taking it as
evidence that he hadn't yet made Emily pregnant.

Of course this happened shortly after I had turned
Emily away. She'd moved out when she started university, but now, Sandra gone, she'd wanted to come
back. Why? And why hadn't I let her? More than once I
entertained the paranoid thought that the appropriation
of Foley must for her have been in part sweet revenge.
I'm not sure whether I still believe this.

Back in the present tense, Foley, whose glass is
nearly empty, though we can't have been here for more
than twenty minutes, is saying, "Interested in another?"

Coming from anyone else of my acquaintance, this
would be an offer to buy the next round. Coming from

Foley, it's an offer to go up to the bar and get the beer if I give him the money for it.

"Sure, why not." Nothing awaits me at home other than some combination of Emily, the Balkan babysitters, the grandchildren, the morning's encyclopaedia article, and the one-quarter-written, much longer piece on Cleary, whose incompletion will no doubt haunt me for weeks to come.

Foley picks up my twenty and moves toward the bar with annoying deliberation, elder statesman of the generation born in 1970.

When he comes back he asks about the kids, pledges to keep his distance until I give him the all-clear, reveals that he's staying with someone he describes only as "a friend," gives me a number. We talk of other things and a simulacrum of the old days begins to form a cocoon over our table as the afternoon drifts on.

Later, having more or less recovered from my two pints – Foley managed three – I'm watching Ryan at soccer. We're at a schoolyard not far from the university, the heat slowly fading, St. John's summer at its most idyllic. I've volunteered for this duty, much to Emily's relief, I think, but for me it's no chore. Boyhood revisited. What a privilege! I pace the sidelines like an NFL coach, oblivious to the parents in their folding chairs and younger siblings underfoot.

Ryan plays with enthusiasm but no discernible talent or sense of the game. True, he's only seven, but some of his teammates demonstrate skill, athleticism, desire, the coach's son inevitably the prime example. The coach is an elementary school phys ed teacher with just the right attitude for these kids, easing them gently into the conventional paradoxes of masculinity. Do what you're told but know when to improvise. Sometimes you face the enemy one-on-one, but you're always part of a team. Have fun, but try hard to win. Such bromides manifest themselves only in trace elements here, but still. The coach's son and two or three others not only know what to do with the ball, they really want to do it. They understand, at some level, the importance of this ritual. The rest of the team – they play seven a side – chase after the ball in a sort of pack, designated positions forgotten despite the incessant, though never overtly critical, reminders shouted by the coach and his assistant.

These men and the other parents are all at least twenty years younger than I am and clearly regard me, possessor not only of a beard, but a grey one at that, as an anomaly. The assistant occasionally calls me "sir" for no reason. He's a sad-looking man with the sharp features I associate with the personae of c & w hurtin' songs. In a few years he'll look like someone who drinks to forget that his wife is cheating on him. The real coach will never have such troubles. Crew-cut and bland-faced, he has the air of a man who will take practical steps to deal definitively with such matters in their earliest stages, or simply not notice them at all.

Ryan touches the ball rarely and usually by accident. Sometimes he surprises with a good solid kick, but the arts of dribbling, passing, and shooting are beyond his ken. Nevertheless he runs hard up and down the field with the others, jumping and screaming when his team scores. Occasionally, though, when the ball comes toward him in the air, he shies away, arm drawn in against his body, in a gesture I'm culturally conditioned to think of as "girlish." So what, I tell myself.

I keep hoping for the breakthrough moment when he might dribble the ball for ten yards, then pass it off smoothly to a teammate. How I'd like him to know that first-time joy, and how I'd like to be there for it. Doing something real you didn't know you could, and knowing you'll be able to do it anytime from then on. But it won't happen today.

A scrum of about six boys surrounds the ball as though it were an exotic animal that might try to make a getaway. Ryan has a good chance to boot it but holds off, waiting for someone else to move in. I resist the impulse to holler at him, knowing it won't help, and, for that matter, not wishing to call attention to myself.

Then he blocks a shot by accident. It hits him in the stomach, quite hard. He looks surprised but doesn't fall down, in fact makes as if to move toward the ball until an alert teammate takes over and nudges it in the direction of the coach's son, who begins an impressive sortie upfield. Good one, Ryan, says the coach. Now get after it. Get after it.

And he does, or tries to, his skinny legs pumping ludicrously in the general direction of manhood.

About then I notice Maureen Finnerty on the opposite sideline, holding a bicycle and staring vaguely at the action on the field, though I have the wacky unverifiable sense that she's been staring at me, willing me to look at her.

What's she doing here? Her only son must be around twenty-three by now. Perhaps she lives in the neighbourhood and was just passing by, out for a pleasant ride. Then she happens to note a bunch of seven-year-olds playing soccer, and as a long-time fan of the game, she stops, then rides the considerable distance to get to the end of the chain-link fence separating the field from the street, and then, distracted by the high calibre of the play, walks her bike absent-mindedly along the far sideline until, by chance, she stops directly across from me.

Either that, or – flattering, naïve, and paradoxically annoying thought – she's stalking me.

I'm not sure how to handle this. I've forgotten how long it's been since Maureen and I have seen each other. And perhaps this *is* some sort of accident. I decide to let her make the move, if one is to be made. I avoid looking in her direction.

At half-time the coach calls the team together. Look at me, he says, his standard opening. Eyes on me. Ryan is one of the most eager to co-operate. He executes a theatrical little jump, landing directly in front of the coach. Then he makes pretend binoculars with his thumbs and index fingers, peering obediently and just possibly satirically through them. The coach ignores him. He talks earnestly about the importance of taking one's time before shooting on goal, of looking for open teammates to pass to – matters that can be of only theoretical interest to Ryan. Yet he pays closer attention than the boys next to him, abandoning the binoculars after a few seconds.

Someone taps my elbow, not particularly gently. I flinch, the gesture disconcertingly close to the one I've mentally criticized Ryan for.

It's Maureen.

"Why," she says, "are you such a dingus-dongus?"

Maureen Finnerty and I had a thing about ten years ago. "Thing" is the word, not "affair," with its spurious aura of romantic sophistication. We were brought together by what in retrospect looks like mutual desperation, she escaping belatedly from an early shotgun marriage, me thrashing forlornly in the wake of Sandra's departure. At a certain point it became evident that Maureen was interested in more than a few months of r & r, and I bolted, metaphorically speaking, for reasons that, to be truthful, remain obscure. I'd been banking on the statistical bedrock that married women never leave their husbands for the first man they commit adultery with; he's supposed to be a trophy, the occasion for a declaration of independence. But Maureen, wouldn't you know, was the exception. Yet it ended amicably, as they say, the generosity of women once again proving itself miraculous. Some women. We moved on, she farther than I did – to the mainland, Montreal in fact, where her hard-won fluency in French was a career asset, and to another, less desperate, man. Ironic echo of Sandra. We stayed in touch for a time, but not for perhaps the last five years.

Now she's saying, "I'm baaack. Ignoring me isn't going to cut it, Hughie."

"Your girlfriend called," Emily informs me slyly, "seeking information about your whereabouts. Did she track you down?"

Encouraging this sort of discussion is not a good idea. I retreat to my study.

She calls after me. "Did she suggest that you trim that scraggly beard?"

"Merlin Kelliher, the protagonist of *Sacrament of Ashes* (1975), like Cleary himself, grows up in St. John's." This one doesn't sound quite so much like bullshit. What more can I say with certainty? It's the books that are important, though – if anything is – not the embedded autobiography. Drop "like Cleary himself." Focus on the novel's reality, the only thing I do know for sure about the man.

In our brief soccer-pitch dialogue, Maureen, after delicately establishing the fact of my current singleness, has made it clear that she's available, having split eternally from the guy she now calls "He who must not be named." We must get together, she said, under more propitious circumstances. Though what, I wonder now, could be more propitious than the celebration of maleness we were then in the midst of? In any case, she has my number, in more ways than one.

In response to her initial probing, I spoke with commendable masculine terseness, at all cost wishing to avoid sounding "needy" – the chronic problem of her ex-husband, I recall.

"There has been no one for some time," I proclaimed, as a disconcerting image of Foley saying the same thing in parallel circumstances flashed through my mind, though Foley would be speaking in a wistful, quasi-elegiac tone designed to melt the heart – or at least, loins – of the addressee. While twirling his 'stache.

The climactic scene of *Sacrament of Ashes*, after the final confrontation between Merlin and his father, is a dream sequence: Merlin running through the pre-dawn,

anonymous and not-quite-right streets of St. John's –
even narrower than in waking life, the buildings closer
together and taller – running towards the harbour,
following the dove in the absurdly pinched strip of sky
visible directly above, the dove surrounded by an aura
that blended olive and purple, both and neither as one
might expect in dreams, ending with Merlin standing
where the Basilica should have been but in the dream
wasn't. The dove fading as the sun rose, Merlin looking
down at the harbour and through the Narrows to the sea
beyond.

In bed, about to drift off, I replay this scene and try,
despite my own critical principles, and unsuccessfully,
to make sense of the connection between Merlin and
Cleary. I'm willing to bet that Alphonsus Cleary had
the sort of dream that could be oversimplified to create
the novel's dream sequence. But in the brief epilogue
after the dream, Merlin leaves for England, in contrast
to Cleary's real-life destination, the North American
mainland. Was Cleary in the novel signalling that his
decision had been the wrong one, turning his back on
his own cultural origins, to say nothing of the source of
the sun, his literary art an elaborate form of second-
guessing himself?

I think of Maureen looking quickly down at my
hand. "Still there, still deformed," I said. "The visible
effect of Original Sin." She chuckled, remembering an
old joke of hers.

Moments later she caught me peeking down her
shirt to the place where the freckled tan becomes white.

"They're still there, too," she said, grinning. "Everything's there, but looser."

CHAPTER THREE

Emily spends a lot of time on the phone, renewing and solidifying connections with those of her friends who've stayed around, remarkably few compared to the limitless numbers she ran with as an undergraduate. They've gone, a diaspora of educated young Newfoundlanders – to Toronto, Ottawa, New York, MIT, Oxford even, the intellectual equivalents of Fort McMurray, there being so little for them here. Those who've stayed are mostly lawyers or civil servants, or married to someone who is. Of course there are exceptions, like Raissa McCloskey, the award-winning, mildly flaky filmmaker who lives just down the way on Long's Hill.

I know most of the voices by now, but there's one I haven't been able to pin down, calling long distance, I suspect, judging by the woman's formal, even slightly hostile tone. Early this evening, three days after my encounter with Foley, she struck again, sounding more belligerent than usual. No hello, just the bald demand: "I want to speak to Emily."

"I think she's around. Shall I tell her who's calling?"

"No."

"No?"

"Just ask her to come to the phone."

"Someone seems to have forgotten the magic word."

"Look. I don't have time for this. I want Emily."

Defeated, I smack the receiver down on the kitchen table and go off to find my daughter. She's upstairs, doing Samantha's bath.

"It's the incredibly rude woman again."

She scrambles to her feet, a tad too eagerly for my liking. Why should she so readily desert one of her children to speak to this no-name virago?

Samantha delivers a groan/whine as she realizes that Grandad will be taking over. Her mouth turns down in a three-year-old's version of the mask of tragedy.

"When is Mummy coming back?"

"She left only five seconds ago."

"Why is it taking her so long?"

I move discreetly out into the hallway, where I can hear Emily better. I feel cheapened by having to do this, eavesdropping on my own daughter, but it seems somehow necessary. This woman is clearly up to no good. I need to be prepared to defend Emily against whatever threatens her. In previous conversations, I've been able to rule out the following: a collection agency, an aggrieved wife, drug dealers, political parties, an angry landlady, a cult. What's left? "Friend" doesn't quite seem to cover it, either.

It's difficult to make out what Emily is saying, but her tone follows a customary pattern: initial monosyllabic coldness, then exclamations ("Omygod no!") or questions which, to my ear, seem never quite to make sense, then unrestrained high-schooly giggles, and finally brief exchanges in the lowered, ostentatiously "confidential" voice that women use when they speak to each other of death, serious illness, or *schadenfreude*-inspiring scandal.

Tonight's instalment is shorter than most. "You too," I hear Emily saying by way of farewell. "You too." Then: "Ryan, your turn for the bath." With Ryan in earshot, she knows I'll find it even more awkward to grill her, not that I'd get anywhere anyway.

The children in bed, Emily keeping her distance (unnecessarily fussing in the kitchen), I retire to my study with a cup of tea, preparing for the evening, which will, for the first time, be featuring Maureen. Preparation means skimming Maureen's book, presented to me with a combination of pride and touching timidity at our one brief meeting since the soccer game, a rushed coffee yesterday at Tim Hortons. Maureen was in the midst of running errands; as of today, she's house-sitting for a maiden aunt who'll be visiting a non-maiden aunt in Toronto for the next couple of weeks. She's been living with various family members for the two weeks or so since coming back from the mainland. She has money saved, so there's no hurry for a job, but she'd like to get her own place soon.

In any case, the field is now clear for us to get together in a private, non-Emily-monitored environment.

Maureen's book. A nice surprise that she's done it, mixed feelings as I begin to grasp what it is. It was her writing that first brought us together, as they say, back when she was a sessional in our department. Having heard that I taught creative writing, she showed up at my office one day with a sheaf – her word, uttered with charming uncertainty – of poems. They tended to feature strong visual imagery which implied a more complex understanding of the world than the narratorial exposition that surrounded it. I got her to chip away at the commentary; the poetry improved as things happened between us on other levels.

When it was over, I was presented with a parting gift, a meticulous description of a stone eagle, elevated in some unspecified public location, stoically peering through a rainstorm: the pedestal, the hardness, the inability to fly all rendered with subtle clues to indicate that the poem was a portrait of You Know Who.

When Maureen passed the book to me yesterday my first impulse was to check the table of contents to see if the eagle poem was there, or indeed anything I could recognize from the old days. She said, "You haven't seen these. They're all in the voice of a woman I made up." Only then did I notice the title: *Liza Speaks Her Mind*. Liza, she explained, is the Liza from "I'se the B'y," the silenced female voice of the nineteenth-century Newfoundland woman, she to whom the fish is brought home by the self-aggrandizing male protagonist, but about whom nothing more is said. "Look, Hughie, I know it sounds weird, but I think I've tapped into something here. Nobody's done the nineteenth-century Newfoundland woman from a serious feminist perspective before. I can't wait to hear what you think."

Now I'll have to tell her. As I flip through the pages I note that all of the poems have "Liza" in the title and Liza as the speaker, describing some incident from daily life glossed with appropriate feminist commonplaces. Liza, it develops, was sexually abused by her father, and physically and emotionally abused by her husband. She gave birth to eight children, six of whom survived. She worked unbelievably long hours at incredibly tedious tasks. Through it all, she managed to evolve a sophisticated analysis of her oppression by the patriarchy. Possessor of a strong sense of morality, she had no illusions about religion: see "The Sermon Liza Would Have Liked to Preach." Further, she was an autodidact, well familiar with the classics of Western tradition: see the section headed "The Books in Skipper's Sea-Chest," including such poems as "Liza Addresses Beatrice," "Liza Corners Caliban," "Liza Shares a Costril of Spruce Beer with Mary Shelley," and so forth.

All of this contrasts with the image of Maureen that I've long cherished, one associated with cheerful sexual plenitude rather than feminist rhetoric. Why couldn't she have written a book called *Cheerful Sexual Plenitude*? Of course this raises the question of the extent to which my cherished image is an eroticized distortion of the real her. ("The 'real her'?" I can hear Eddie Laskowski asking derisively. Yes, Eddie, there is a real her. That proposition must be true because you believe the contrary, okay?)

It's not that Maureen's poems are bad, exactly. It's rather that the concept seems somehow unworthy of her, outdated, second-rate. There's something sad about the whole business, despite the glossy cover with its stylized faux-naïve image of a big-assed woman toiling at a flake, courtesy of an obscure local artist.

In places there are flashes of something else, though: in "Liza Smells Like Fish," for example, with its sly paralleling of woman and fish as equally commodified, to use the current academic vernacular. And there's "Liza's Unspoken Love Poem":

> You belong in me
> Like a tongue in a mouth.
> A cod's tongue.
> A salivating mouth.

I laughed out loud when I first read it, but now I'm not sure why – the wit of the parody, or the idea that the Atwood poem is worth parodying. Possibly both. Mixed feelings, as I say.

At fifty-eight, am I justified in lying in order to get laid? This is the deep moral question I'm wrestling with when the phone rings again. Emily, always quick on the telephone draw, answers before I can react, but, anomalously, this one's for me.

"Hey, perfesser," the voice says, the mispronunciation deliberate and venerable, a thirty-year-plus-old standing joke. It's Ray McGuire, university buddy, *mon semblable, mon frère*, calling from Ottawa. It's been months since we spoke. He did a degree in economics at Carleton, went into the civil service, and now makes twice my salary helping inept entrepreneurs sell their stuff abroad. He's good natured about the flack he takes from me regarding his dual role as espouser of free enterprise values and front man for a *dirigiste* bureaucracy, distributing goodies to those philosophically opposed to big government.

"Listen, I've got something for you on this Cleary guy." Ray has followed my academic career as though it were a spectator sport, reading every obscure publication of mine that I tell him about. God knows how skewed his idea of contemporary literature must be. Now he's particularly interested in Cleary, because of the Ottawa connection. "I met this ex-Oblate who says he knew him. They lived in the same residence over on Springdale or Springfield, whatever it is. Says he thinks Cleary may be alive, or at least was for a while after he disappeared. Says he was sick of being a priest, plus there was some kind of problem with the hierarchy, some 'animosity' was the word he used, between Cleary and his bosses. He was vague about it, but I think I can get more out of him next time."

"Next time?"

"Yeah, he's a baseball fan, this guy, and I've got some Lynx tickets for next week, said he'd come with me, so I'll see what I can get for you."

I'm touched. There's no point in explaining that Cleary is so unimportant that no one else on the planet cares if he's dead or alive. "So where did you meet this guy?"

A slight hesitation. "A support group. For parents of kids with problems. He's got one too."

I recall that teenaged Danny has for years been nothing but trouble. I mumble something sympathetic.

"It's like everything we do is wrong."

I picture him clearly, if inaccurately. He's talking into a cordless phone in the backyard shed he uses as a workshop, his face expressing genial bafflement undercut by pain.

"I can't figure it out."

"What's he been up to?"

"Let me just tell you something first, just to illustrate. He was in jail for a week because of this thing

I'm going to tell you about. So then his hearing comes up, and I have to go down. Madge and I both go to this group, Hopewood it's called, this guy Rick Blackburn runs it? The guy who used to have the smoked meat place and knew all the politicians, always on TV? Anyway, now he's set up this group for parents, and they say, Don't bail him out, let him stay in jail, that's the only way. So I go down to the court, it's night court, right, and I went to see the judge. I'd been told I could see him half an hour before it started. I wanted to talk to him about what the options were. So I go in to where the judge's office is, and this guy, the bailiff I guess, says, yes, I can see the judge just before court starts, but then he doesn't show up until five minutes before it's supposed to start and then says there isn't time to see him in his office. You still listening, perfesser?"

"Yep. Keep going." This has always been a feature of our conversations, tolerance of the extended monologue. It's been a long time, though.

"Okay, so he says, You just have to sign for him and there's no problem. So I said, Look, I don't want to sign for him, that's what I wanted to see you about. We're in the hallway outside the courtroom, right, the judge is this little French guy with a mustache, and he just explodes. I mean he goes ballistic. He says, Look, I have the cops bring him in all the way from Innes Road, and now you say you don't want to sign for him? And I said, I never asked to have him brought *in* from Innes Road. I wanted to talk to you about options. As far as I'm concerned he should stay out at Innes Road. And he said, I had him brought in from Innes Road because you were supposed to sign for him. All you have to do is sign. And I said,

There's a misunderstanding here, I wanted to talk about options. And he said, I'm not going to ask the cops to take him all the way back to Innes Road. So I ended up signing for him. Even something as simple as that gets screwed up."

And so on, through a series of sad vignettes from his son's recent past, until Ray circles back to the question of what Danny had done to be at Innes Road in the first place.

"He and his buddies were in Pinecrest Cemetery, and there was this lady there at the grave of her three-year-old daughter, and they grab her purse and get her car keys and take off in her car. And even then he could've got out of it. The police wanted to talk to him, they weren't even going to arrest him, they just wanted him to come in so they could talk to him about it, and he said, If they want to talk to me they can come and arrest me. So of course they did. That's the way he is."

Ray pauses here, giving me the chance to chime in with a few clichés, embarrassed at their inadequacy. We move away from the topic of Danny as delicately as we can. Finally Cleary comes up again. "One other thing this guy told me about him. He was a big John Prine fan. Used to call the residence the Hotel Bolderado. Is that helpful?"

"It could explain a lot."

And we wind down from there, the sadness gently merging with nostalgia for the days when we'd drink draft beer in shabby downtown Ottawa taverns, engaging in rambling dialogues in which nothing needed to be concealed or defended.

On the short drive to Maureen's temporary abode, I allow some of the good memories to surface, though I know – I think – how dangerous that might be. Hughie and Maureen's Greatest Erotic Hits. Golden Oldies from the early nineties. But of course all is (probably) changed, changed utterly.

At the same time, I register the irony: I'm driving along a street called Merrymeeting. Honest to God. I have no idea of the history of the name, but there it is, a thoroughfare designed for the express purpose of bringing people together for joyous messing about. Maybe things will be the same after all.

And why shouldn't they be? Let's bring back that old roguish conspiracy, Hughie and Maureen against the world. Both of us in self-imposed pastoral exile from the city-state of marital normality – she: extra-; me: post-. Both of us with the naïveté of sixteen-year-olds with the family car, a full tank, and the open, blue-skied road before us. Example: we used no contraception, totally unnecessary she said, since her tubes were tied, a phrase that always evoked for me an image of a pair of grey, sausage-like objects yoked violently together by an incongruous twist-tie at the top. As for STDs, she'd been faithful to Ken since their marriage in 1976, as he'd been to her, she thought – though evidence to the contrary would eventually be forthcoming. My story was that I'd been faithful to Sandra (icon of fidelity herself) with maybe one minor, demonstrably harmless infraction on my part. So there we were, completely in the clear.

Trust, we called it.

No reason we can't get it back, is there? By now I'm

off Merrymeeting, navigating through the maze of mostly one-way streets that comprise the neighbourhood of Georgestown. The bogus Odysseus closes in on his hometown, where Penelope waits in horny anticipation. I recall Maureen's innocent delight in receiving oral sex, the desire signalled, as she strode out of the bathroom, by the brightly delivered line: "It's clean." Ah, the expectant smile, the tits bouncing gently, a confident citizen of the democratic republic of pleasure, asking for no more than her birthright. On the bed, opening her legs, offering pretty much everything. Trust.

That was then, I remind myself as I approach the door. I feel the need for a snappy opening, as if this were a performance of some kind – which perhaps, unsettling thought, it is. "The eagle has landed?" But she might not remember the poem, or, indeed, the event. She would have been about twelve when the Americans went to the moon.

I settle for parody of a hypothetical wide-eyed poetry fan: "Hey, you look just like your picture on the book I saw in Chapters." It's not quite true, but I want to demonstrate willingness to deal with the book early on. In the photo she's wearing glossy lipstick and a school-marmy white blouse buttoned up to her chin, odd combination of primness and sexual come-on (those lips dominate the foreground), not likely to be deliberate on the part of her publisher. In real life she's not wearing make-up, which I take as a compliment, no need to disguise anything.

What you see is what you might get.

"So," she's saying, "it's you" – as though the public versions of the last couple of days were mere simulacra, bearing only incidental resemblance to the now-present real me.

"Yup."

We're not going to embrace. She's wearing a summery-looking dress, pale yellow the main colour, modest scoop at the neckline, hem inches below the knee. She takes evasive action, backing out of the tiny vestibule into the main hallway.

"Come on in. Sit down. Let's have a look at you."

She ushers me – the gesture deserves the formality of that word – into the living room, which seems cramped with miscellaneous items of furniture encrusted with a heavy overlay of knickknacks. I try to settle into an armchair that looks more comfortable than it is. Maureen sits on a tiny sofa opposite, knees ostentatiously locked together beneath the fabric of the dress.

We talk about nothing much. We're boxers in the first round of a championship fight, flicking harmless jabs, watching how quickly the other guy reacts. Maybe Maureen is as uncertain as I've suddenly become. She suggests we go for a drive. "It'll be like old times."

This is a reference to the fact that we seemed to spend a lot of time in cars driving aimlessly or to unlikely, randomly chosen local destinations, on the theory that Ken would have trouble closing in on a moving, unpredictable target. Those were the days, all right.

As soon as we're belted in, she says, "So what do you think of Liza?"

I try to tell her, as diplomatically as I can, what I think. It's only when I start to speak that I realize I'm not going to lie.

"So you hate it."

"No. No. But you're kind of spelling things out more directly than a lot of poetry does."

"I knew you'd say something like that."

Thank God, she doesn't sound hurt or angry.

"Good old Hughie. Show, don't tell. Let the image speak for itself. A veritable compendium of creative writing proverbs." That "veritable compendium" is mockery aimed at what she once, half-jokingly but only half, identified as my "pedantic" conversational style.

"Yep, Liza does tend to run her mouth, doesn't she? But see, I wanted her to be accessible. The stuff I was writing back then was for posterity or something, not for people. Present company excepted, ha-ha. This stuff, I wanted people to be able to use it."

The car seems to have a mind of its own. We're going to go up Signal Hill, it has somehow informed me. Maureen hasn't commented, so I guess it's all right with her.

"High school girls, say. Maybe they need to have things spelled out for them. Things about how they have access to a strength nobody tells them about. That's what poetry is for, art is for."

This carries such conviction that it moves me. But at the same time – and here's another quick reprise of the old Maureen – she is herself amused at the extent to which she's getting carried away, as indicated by the concluding giggle, which sounds too spontaneous to be self-deprecating. "You'll laugh at this, too, Hughie, but the best thing that could happen to me as a poet is to get into a high school textbook."

I keep my eyes on the road – we're heading up Signal

Hill now, passing the Battery Hotel – but I can imagine the defiant "so there" look she's directing at me.

"And you? What're you up to?"

"What is this, a job interview?"

"Maybe."

The parking lot is nearly full. It's a warm, clear evening, and there are lots of tourists. We walk along the path at the end opposite to the Tower. And it strikes me that we've been here before, many times, and that this whole outing is apparently a matter of reflexes kicking in, something neither of us is inclined to question.

"The sea is calm tonight," I say with the sort of pompous intonation that Foley would doubtless give it. When did I start to sound like Foley?

"Yes, b'y, we'll be true to one another," Maureen says, laughing. It was as much a joke *in illo tempore*, too, or so I thought.

Still, something has changed. I'm on probation. Maureen steers the conversation back to what I'm now, professionally, "up to." The encyclopaedia article completed, I've now gone back to working on the second, longer Cleary project of the summer, a 15,000-word piece for a volume in a series called *Contemporary Canadian Novelists*, a sort of academically respectable version of *Coles Notes*, though who would actually need such material on Cleary is a question not easily answered. The assignment courtesy of the editor, Jack Goldham, an old office mate from grad school, who confessed that he'd never heard of Cleary, but if I was keen on it, he'd make room....

"So why are you interested in this guy?"

"The strange voice, the intellectualism, the weirdly

heretical ideas, the energy and passion, the combination of all that and being a priest interests me. And I like the idea that there's a coherent, or at least not totally incoherent, interpretation of the world animating the writer's vision. However wacky the interpretation is."

We've climbed a short flight of wooden steps to the top of the bare rocky hillock where Maureen and I first kissed. Or maybe the second or third time. But the mood isn't right for that to be mentioned, never mind trying for a replay.

"Wacky?"

"Yes, because even if you disagree with whatever you take the author's position to be, at least there's an acknowledgement that reality consists of more than social and psychological facts. That interests me."

"Why?"

We're staring out at the sea, the sky rapidly darkening now. Something perverse about facing east when the sun is setting, as though attention is owed not to the sun's quixotic rearguard action but rather to the featureless big battalions of the night.

"Good question. It just seems more in keeping with what an artist should do – there should be something more than a record of how people spoke and what they did and what they thought in a certain cultural context."

"Spoken like a true romantic."

I decide to let the subject drop, before she construes my position as an implicit attack on her poetry – which, come to think of it, it is, more or less.

But then she surprises me.

"Actually, I'm thinking maybe my own work should move in that direction. Maybe Liza is a dead end."

"But didn't you say, back down the hill there …"

"Yeah, but I don't completely believe it. I mean, Liza should get her fifteen minutes of fame in the textbooks, but wouldn't that be enough?"

"You had me fooled."

"Not a difficult feat, evidently."

As we walk back toward the parking lot, I tell her about my troubles with Emily.

"It's obvious," Maureen says. "She's discovered she's gay."

"What?" This is the possibility I'd rather not confront, no doubt an index of my lack of enlightenment. Disenlightenment?

"The phone call. That woman is her lover, or wants to be. But you must have known that at some level. That's what she's running from, not Terry Foley."

I'm not quite convinced. My daughter the lesbian. Shouldn't there have been clues? But maybe there were. Her forthrightly expressed sympathy, from high school on, for the cause of gay rights, something I put down to her general – and to me, welcome – liberal mindset. An old school friend's coming out of the closet proclaimed in terms of fervent approval. Still, that's not much to go on.

"Don't worry, Hughie. You'll get over it." We're back in the car now. She reaches over, pats my hand like an older sister.

At that moment it becomes evident that, without prejudice as to what might happen in the future, there will for an absolute certainty be no sex tonight. Something about the precisely defined nature of the physical contact. Maureen's hand does not linger, does not move a millimetre from the point where the fingers touch down, instead heading straight up and out, no opportunity for my knuckles to nestle suggestively in her palm, or for me to redeploy my entire hand for a quick, possibly extendable squeeze of hers.

It can't be that she's put off by the deformity. We crossed that bridge long ago.

I feel annoyance at the withholding of what I thought had been unequivocally promised. Perhaps she's uncertain about how to proceed, what sort of treaty needs to be negotiated.

But also at another (deeper?) level I'm starting to feel a kind of revulsion about the whole thing, not quite the old-time religion of Sartrean nausea but maybe a sort of nausea-lite, no danger of real despair, more like a virtual reality version. In the end, do I really care whether I have sex with this woman, or whether we go on to have a "relationship," a word I can remember us laughing at? Isn't there something unseemly about a man of my age hoping for a quick fuck – or an indefinite series of them – something sad, something that makes one wish to turn away, stifling the impulse to retch, as he forces his hairy sagging body toward that most traditional and banal of destinations?

As we're gliding out of the parking lot, there's Terry Foley walking hand in hand with a woman I've never seen before. I get only a glimpse. She's tall, sharp-featured, wears glasses, has long dark hair arranged in ringlets, something that for reasons unknown I associate with biblical sluttiness, the sort of woman the Book of Proverbs warns us against. Foley and I make eye contact momentarily. I can see his eyebrows begin to rise as I make the turn to head downhill.

On the drive back to Maureen's place, neither of us says much. I'm wondering if something can be done to redeem the evening, what it would take to give it some shape or point. I'm mildly surprised when she invites me in for a beer.

"*One* beer, my son, and then it's off you go."

Three beers later we're finally hitting it off, not so much because of the alcohol as because of the subject matter: our time together, who we were back then and how we got there, never mind who we think we are now. Maureen, I realize, knows a frightening amount about me. I've confided things to her about my marriage that not only have I told no one else, but actually have forgotten until Maureen refers to them casually. But mainly she wants to autopsy Us, with a capital U. And this, I come to understand, has been the main item on the evening's agenda all along. She wants the truth.

"Let me get this straight," she's saying much later, sandals kicked off, but legs demurely curled under her on the sofa. "The gospel according to St. Hughie. Geography. The world is flat. It ends at the edge of the bed. Beyond that is the abyss. Cosmology. We willed this world into existence. While we're in it, we remember nothing outside. We speculate about nothing beyond it. How'm I doing? Have I got it right? Oh, and above all, and this is really important, no comparisons are to be made. Right?" The tone is not accusatory, exactly. And she's enjoying her own cleverness. But she does want a response, something real.

"You've learned well. That is what I was preaching. Back then."

She sips her beer, peers across at me. "Can't be that way again, H-man."

This pisses me off a tad. She's traditionally used "H-man" the way that Brits use "Sunshine," to rebuke and/or patronize someone close.

"What way can it be?"

"Oh, he's bristling. We'll work on it. But not tonight."

"Just don't call me H-man."

"Deal."

The kitchen at midnight. Emily would not be pleased to learn that I drove the short distance home after three beers, but she's probably been asleep for more than an hour. Perhaps a medicinal dose of cognac would be in order. As I pour, I consider the signs of Emily's invasion. The garbage bag filled to overflowing, a misguided economy measure. On the counter an open two-litre ice cream container half-filled with banana peels, eggshells, tea bags, salad detritus: Emily's composting project. There's something unhealthy and defiant about the way Emily has approached this business, as though she wants to rub everyone's nose in the gross physicality of everyday existence. The container is beside the sink, in close proximity to the area where meals are prepared. The Balkan babysitters are puzzled, and, I sense, slightly dismayed by this arrangement. It's been a struggle, Emily has told me, to get them to recognize that certain substances are to be carefully preserved and placed in the container. They think they know "garbage" when they see it.

It's as though Emily is saying, Once you didn't want me in your house. Now I'm going to show you how a house should be run.

I briefly contemplate sabotage, but I know the game wouldn't be worth the candle. Should Emily find out, she'd be angry, and, worse, hurt. And I wish that she experience no more hurt, my daughter, my darling daughter.

Chapter Four

I wake up with a sense of unsubstantiated yet profound revelation.

Emily has committed a crime.

Where does this idea come from? I've decided that I simply don't believe Maureen's discovery-of-lesbian-identity theory. So now, all the obvious possibilities having been side-lined, the unexpected truth has been allowed to emerge. Of course I don't know it's truth in any sense except the most important, the kind that doesn't require evidence.

Still, there's the issue of what to do next. Confrontation, thirty years of Emily-watching suggests, is unlikely to be fruitful.

My daughter has committed a crime. Emily as Raskolnikov, gratuitously offing an old lady or two? No, it would have to have been committed out of principle. And she's retreated to St. John's and the safety of yours truly because? She feels guilty and wants a clean slate, or at least a place where she can believe the slate is perceived to be clean. Or she's afraid she'll be found out, tracked down, brought to justice, and fleeing the scene of the crime is the best tactical move. Or some combination of the above.

And behind or beneath that, my original rejection of her as post-Sandra housemate. She's giving me a second chance. Or she's come expecting (wanting?) a second rejection to confirm her darkest theories about my unkindness, my parental inadequacy. And why did I turn her away? The details are unclear at this distance. She represented a link to Sandra that I wished to sever. While officially neutral, she was certainly her mother's ally. No doubt she'd be reporting on my every move, not that that would have mattered all that much, come to think of it. If she'd been two years younger, she would have left St. John's with Sandra, started university in Ontario.

As for me, I think I wanted "freedom," something I was sure her presence would impair. Nothing personal, except of course for her that's exactly what it was. So the seeds of our current communications impasse were sown. We've learned to converse like diplomats, careful to let no damaging word slip out.

How I wish we could get beyond this.

But what exactly did she do in Vancouver and why? It occurs to me that while I'd swear Emily is a person whose every significant act is in some way informed by her principles, I'd be hard pressed to identify any of them.

Coterminous with this insight, indeed pushing it aside as I begin to replay last night, is the bleak memory of Maureen asserting that we'll have to "work on it," the pronoun referring to the mercifully unstated noun "relationship."

Image of the two of us as Egyptian slaves somehow bound together in the midst of a group of hundreds hauling huge blocks of stone toward a pyramid construction site. Heat, thirst, backache.

Me: Why are we doing this, again?

Maureen (a dreamy look of devotion transforming her face instantaneously): We are privileged to be building the pyramid of our god-king Relationship. Let us toil assiduously in his service. Our lives may be sacrificed, but let us labour joyfully, for we are as nothing before his glory.

I notice that back in Egypt neither of us is wearing much, that Maureen is sporting some not-fully-imagined shapeless garment on the upper part of her body, which allows me a good view of most of her left breast, the colour – we're Egyptians, after all – of a deep bronze tan. She catches me looking (a reprise of our meeting at the soccer field?) and shifts ever so slightly to allow a quick glimpse of succulent nipple accompanied by a complicit wink, giving me hope that the god-king may yet manifest himself in our own humble flesh ....

("Succulent?" I ought to be ashamed.)

This foolishness is brought to an end by screams from downstairs, where Samantha has, for perhaps the fourth consecutive morning, been found guilty of eating raisins from her Raisin Bran while declaring herself a conscientious objector with respect to the consumption of the bran itself. Emily – on principle, I'm pretty sure – has decided that Raisin Bran is what is best for Samantha, and that should be that.

Samantha doesn't think so. There are basic issues of human dignity here, her wailing suggests. Sandra begat Emily who begat Samantha. Three generations of female stubbornness, all of it highly principled.

Time to face the day.

The spectre of *Contemporary Canadian Novelists* hovers over my desk. I should not be staring out the window. I should be writing a brief but pithy – and above all, readable! – plot summary of Cleary's second novel, the ironically titled *Isle of the Blessed* (1977). Why am I doing this? Not a question I spend much time entertaining. It's as though Father Cleary and I are spousally attached, our conjugal union so long-established there's no point in exploring its origins. Even death hasn't permitted us to part.

If, in fact, there's been a death.

Isle of the Blessed features an unnamed first-person protagonist who seems to be a disaffected Irish monk in an unidentified century, a carefully contrived amalgam of everything from the fourteenth to the eighteenth. The monk is shipwrecked on a desolate-seeming but inhabited island – or perhaps he is not shipwrecked, perhaps he has deliberately left a passing ship in the hope that the island is uninhabited: the ambiguously written page-long introduction leaves both possibilities open.

The time it takes me to get this far seems inordinately long. The mystery of Emily's conjectured crime bobs unrelentingly up to the surface of my consciousness as I try to focus on the bleak landscape of Cleary's nameless island. It's tempting to try to instigate an old-fashioned father-daughter heart-to-heart, but I know that any such dialogue would quickly morph into something out of Beckett.

Me: We can't go on like this, not talking about it.
Emily: Not talking about what?
Me: I think you know.
Emily: I have no idea what you mean.
Me: No idea at all?
Emily: None whatsoever.
Me: Are you sure?

And sooner or later this bit of engaging stichomythia would be disrupted by the entrance of Pozzo and Lucky, as played by Ryan and Samantha. I would not be able to bring myself to express my suspicions directly. To do so would be counterproductive. Emily would exit calmly, stage left, and I'd be sitting there, alone. Like Krapp.

Perhaps Sandra would be of some help here, since – as with so much – Sandra is the original, Emily the mass-producible knockoff: the reticence, the hoarding up of emotional toxicity whose presence is detectable in body language, and in curt speech, affectless in tone, minor gestures like the not-quite-slamming but louder-than-necessary closing of cupboard doors, the refusal to make eye contact. Followed by not, as might be expected, an explosion, but what I hypothesize to be an *im*plosion, a sucking in of negative energy, papered over by bright-eyed, smiling determination to carry on as normal. Sandra, however, did occasionally explode. Perhaps it was having to witness such events that made Emily decide at an early age that to explode is to be uncool.

As for me, I'm tranquility personified under pretty much all circumstances. Or so I like to think. I will not confront Emily. I will proceed cautiously, investigating leads. Only so far there aren't any. This evening I will phone Sandra to see if she too has identified Emily as a perp. She would never volunteer such information, fearing ridicule or simply not trusting me, but if I make the first move she might be forthcoming, indeed might take some minor pleasure in demonstrating that she knows or intuits more than I do. After all these years, she still might do that.

The simplicity of Cleary's neatly designed world draws me back into it. The island appears to include elements of the Falklands, Tristan da Cunha, the Aleutians, and Easter Island, minus the statues. The inhabitants are of vaguely delineated but clearly non-European ethnicity. They treat the monk neither as god nor demon. In fact, their rudimentary religion has no place for such melodramatic figures, instead resembling a sort of mild pantheism. It doesn't occur to them to question where he has come from. He's immediately accepted as one of their own. Indeed, they have no concept of anyone who is not "one of their own."

I plod onward. The things that really interest me, language, tone, the sardonic persona of the monk, are not likely to be of interest to my potential reader, described in the marching orders sent out by *Contemporary Canadian Novelists* as "an intelligent but possibly unsophisticated undergraduate." In the case of my essay, though, there is something deeply disingenuous about positing any reader at all. Cleary's books have been out of print for at least twenty years. No instructor will ever put one on a syllabus. I've been commissioned to write this thing only because Jack Goldham, the series editor, was my office mate in grad school. So my only real audience is me.

Of course I'll be able to put it on my CV.

What interests me about the tone is the combination of intellectual arrogance and a genuine-seeming sense of wonder, dismissive superiority juxtaposed with naïve exuberance, though how this quality can be analyzed escapes me. Probably I'll settle for quoting a couple of paragraphs and gushing about them. My hypothetical target audience would simply skip over them and move on to the next salient point about character or theme, no doubt defacing the relevant passages with their ubiquitous yellow markers, whose presence seems always to carry with it an unintended allusion to urine. Is it too harsh to think of these earnest youngsters as so many dogs, marking off their territory? Probably. My view is, no doubt, jaundiced. I've been at this too long.

The monk quickly learns the islanders' language, becomes a member of the community. The main food source is fish. The islanders spend an inordinate amount of time and energy in their boats, always seeming to catch just enough to allow their society to survive from one year to the next, in a perpetual state of cheerful collective near-exhaustion. The monk suggests an improvement in the design of the nets. The islanders agree to give it a try, and it works. The new, larger nets fill quickly, though the average size of the individual fish becomes somewhat smaller. The monk is hailed in a low-key way as a hero. For the first time in living memory, food is available in abundance. What used to be a long day's catch can now be hauled in in less than an hour. The islanders are ready to explore the experience of leisure, and they have the monk to thank for it. This takes us to page 60 of 210.

The university is sunk deep in its customary midsummer coma. The flags in front of the Administration Building slouch at half-mast, no doubt as a show of mourning for some recently deceased employee. Or is it Hopkins's Mar-gar-et we mourn for, the slow demise of the university itself? The departed person, if faculty, will not be replaced. Probably another five of us would have to bite the dust for someone new to be hired.

The English department is moribund. Secretarial staff seem to outnumber my colleagues, only one or two of whom may be glimpsed behind their half-open office doors or sighted on aimless-seeming forays along the corridors. Somewhere classes are being held, but few students are to be seen here; they have the out-of-place look of extras who've showed up at the set too early or too late.

On the way to my office, I'm intercepted by a familiar voice. "Step inside, will you, professor."

It's Barney Power, or more properly, Dr. Barnabus Power, Ph.D., as it says on his door. Barney is a huge, ponderous, good-hearted, gloomy, irrational man of approximately my age, one of a slowly dwindling band of Newfoundlanders who teach in the department, dwindling since the day it was decided that searches for tenure-track positions had to be advertised nationally.

When Barney speaks, much of the time "th" becomes "d."

"Close the door."

Immediately I know this has to do with the race for the headship. I have an idea which side he's on. The contestants are Alice Plover and Reg Pike. I've noticed that in conversation about their candidacies, both have become cartoon-like versions of their flesh-and-blood selves. Thus Alice, who's plugged away single-mindedly to establish an interdisciplinary medieval studies program, is now characterized as "ruthless," "narrowly ambitious," and "out for herself," as though that last couldn't as well be said about the rest of us. And Reg, a Victorianist with an impressive publication record, is now a "self-absorbed pedant" who would cause the department to slide into perdition through sloppy paperwork and (get this) "lack of people skills," as though that, too, couldn't be said about almost everyone else. Barney, to the best of my knowledge, has no use for either of them.

"Rest your holy and blessed," he says.

This is an allusion to a story he's told me more than once about a bishop visiting an outharbour parish, the punchline having to do with a local, poorly briefed "youngfella" who invited the bishop to sit down and rest his "holy and blessed arse." When I don't laugh at his jokes, Barney will mock me for what he takes to be my squeamishness at the prospect of being seen to laugh at Newfoundlanders. But it's not excessive political correctness; often the stories simply aren't funny.

And there are other stories, sad ones, about his long-abandoned career as a musician, which had its heyday during his time as a doctoral student in Dublin some thirty years ago. He was a drummer in a rock band, he will explain, torn between his scholarly vocation and his pursuit of stardom. "I made the wrong choice," he will say sadly. The band went on to achieve the scaled-down Irish version of fame. Barney will cast himself in a role analogous to that of the Fifth Beatle, except – as he will insist each time he tells the story – his departure from the group was voluntary. The life of a professor in an obscure North American university has turned out to be pretty small potatoes compared to what might have been.

There's a large map of Ireland on the wall behind his desk. Many times over the years, on my way to teach "The Dead," I've stopped by to be reminded of where the Bog of Allen is.

Sometimes, for Barney, "th" becomes simply "t," then morphs into "d" in the next word.

"I think that Alice has the potential to mellow."

This is news. What could Barney hope to gain from a Plover headship? And surely he knows in his heart that no matter who wins, within weeks he'll be complaining about him or her.

"Is there any evidence of mellowing?"

Barney's response is standard. He simply ignores the question.

"I think that Alice has demonstrated the potential to mellow considerably," he says, increasing the volume slightly. He has, his tone suggests, carefully considered my request for evidence and found it irrelevant for reasons too sophisticated for me to understand.

"Further, I don't think Reg is up to the job."

I'm not quite dumb enough to ask why. Reg is a Newfoundlander. But not a Catholic. He's a townie and Barney is from around the bay.

"You know who's supporting Reg, don't you?"

Actually I don't. "I assume it's the anti-union crowd, since Reg crossed the line." A reference to our brief, shining brothers-and-sisters moment of two or three years back, when we hit the bricks, faced down the administration goons, and struck a blow for workers everywhere. Or something like that.

Barney appears to mull this over. But, no surprise, I'm not to be given credit for minimal perspicacity.

"Lady Bickerstaff," he says. "Bernadette O'Keefe."

Double perfidy. Victoria Bickerstaff is a Brit, annoyance enough in itself even if it weren't for the fact that the Bickerstaffs are known to be practising Anglicans. Barney's loathing of Bernadette is of a different stripe, its origins murky, the reasons for its survival even more so. Ask politely for a bill of particulars and you'll get a brief litany of Bernadette's actually quite mild eccentricities and examples of over-favourable treatment she's been given by previous heads and deans, culminating in her recent promotion to full professor, a rank to which Barney does not himself aspire. "How has she managed to get where she is?" he will ask, shaking his head as though the answer were both too well known and too turpitudinous to merit articulation.

Reg Pike. An Anglican and a Newfoundlander, most unnatural coupling of proper nouns, as far as Barney is concerned. It's not exactly that he believes that Newfoundland is Ireland, rather that there should be, ideally, no significant difference between the two. And here's Reg, non-practising religionist but very actively practising townie-with-connections, who is, as noted, a prolific publisher. "Too many publications," Barney will say, implying that he, Barney, has aimed at quality rather than the vulgarity of quantity, and if his career has suffered because of it, that is a price worth paying. Finally, Reg once made what Barney considers to be a slighting reference to his, Barney's home community. In print.

"Reg Pike is a nasty man. If Reg Pike becomes head, you can be sure that things will get very unpleasant around here. As if they weren't unpleasant enough already."

No telling what Barney thinks that might mean. The power of the head is actually quite limited. In days of yore we've had much worse than Reg or Alice, and survived.

I tell Barney, truthfully, that I've been considering voting for Reg (mainly because Plover is a dimwit), knowing that this will unearth some hitherto concealed nugget of marginally accurate rumour. As I begin to enumerate Reg's virtues, he stares at some point behind my right shoulder, blatantly tuning me out. He's not merely pretending, playfully, to be rudely not listening. He really is rudely not listening, the only educated adult I know who is somehow allowed to do this. God knows how much university-related bullshit he's been able to screen out over the years.

It's unlikely that the danger of solipsism has occurred to him.

He waits until I've finished, then says, "And another thing about your man. Ask Bill Duffett. That's all I'll say. Just ask Bill Duffett. But don't tell him I told you to."

"Okay, Barney, I will. I mean, I won't. I will and I won't, in that order."

"And you'll keep the faith, will you?"

There's an envelope taped to my office door, the handwriting purple with many loops. As I suspect, it turns out to be from Raissa McCloskey, former student of mine and current friend of Emily, and "one of Canada's most exciting younger filmmakers," according to a recent – and only mildly patronizing – *Globe & Mail* profile.

In the note she explains that she has important information to impart to me about Emily. On no account is Emily to be allowed to know that she has contacted me. Emily has told her that I go to the university every day: hence this method of communication. Don't call her from home, in case Emily should overhear. Perhaps we could meet downtown tomorrow morning for coffee? If I can't make it, call or email from my office – she hasn't dared to email this message, lest Emily be looking over my shoulder if I should read it from my computer at home.

"Please," she concludes, "keep this between you and I." Signed with a large round dot over the "i" in Raissa, a dot containing, on close inspection, a tiny perfect smiley-face.

Is this serendipity, or straight-up synchronicity? Either way, I'm starting to feel that a mystery, though possibly a sorrowful one, is capable of being solved. And that makes me feel, in a suitably reserved and ironically nuanced way, good.

Back on Cleary's island, the monk finds that he now has

a certain amount of unasked-for power over the lives of his new compatriots. What should they do with their newfound leisure?

The monk, in need of amusement himself, has a few ideas. He introduces the islanders to the notion of games, theatre, poetry, ritual. They respond with delight. In places Cleary (via his monk) brilliantly evokes the joy and mystery of the islanders' first attempts to make art, the prose becoming uncharacteristically near-purplish before inevitably turning ironic a sentence or two later. In such passages I discern a pristine version of Cleary that might once have been the major or primary one, and that has somehow survived the descent into adulthood, in however atrophied a form.

Of course this information will be of no use to the hyper-naïve reader of *Contemporary Canadian Novelists*.

The monk's next move is to incorporate the new leisure activities into the daily lives of the islanders, at the same time introducing another pastime – the moral evaluation of their behaviour. Until this point, their morality has been a matter of acting intuitively, not in accordance with an interpretation of principles or rules. But now the monk provides names, definitions, illustrations – avarice, hope, lust, charity, temperance, gluttony, fortitude; the whole panoply of Western virtues and vices now becomes, as it were, available for use.

And the use to which it is put is essentially recreational. The monk teaches the islanders that the purpose of using moral terms to interpret their lives is not to encourage them to strive for perfection, an impossible goal, but rather to help them achieve a balance in their actions between positive and negative, good and evil. To this end he devises an elaborate system of scoring. An individual's performance is measured by a combination of self-evaluation and the judgment of others. Sometimes it is necessary for someone to cause someone else to suffer in order to improve his score, the sufferer himself gaining points for forgiveness. The islanders are scrupulously honest in all such matters; there is, after all, no tradition of corruption which might influence them.

They take great delight in their new life. Innovation is applauded. Precise evaluation of the morality of specific acts becomes the province of a council of elders. An annual festival is held to honour those whose actions are statistically closest to an ideal balance.

The monk chooses to wield no authority over the community. He lives among them as an ordinary citizen, seeking no special privileges. Harmony reigns, though of course in a sense it already has. Years pass. The monk grows old.

As for the fishing, the new nets continue to function efficiently, though year by year the catch grows slightly smaller. But such is the abundance that no one is concerned.

We're up to page 137 now. Several hundred words of plot summary. Which passes, in my profession, for a morning's work.

And no one, ever, will read it with enthusiasm or delight.

The supper hour comes and goes, the kids are manoeuvred bedward, Emily herself retires early, claiming exhaustion. I have resisted the temptation to mention Raissa McCloskey's name to her.

Near midnight the phone rings.

"Hello, it's Sandra."

Sawndra. Over thirty years in this country, and that aah-sound has remained constant. Give her credit, grudgingly.

"Sandra," I say, exaggerating the aah. "How are you?"

"Well, thank you. How is she?"

"Okay, I guess. Did you want to speak to her? She's already gone to bed."

"No, actually. I wanted your … your perspective." The hesitation is caused by her unwillingness to acknowledge that I could have something as impressive-sounding as a perspective. "If you have time. If it's not too inconvenient." The second syllable given slightly more than its due in a vestigial North-of-England way.

"Not at all," I say, hammering away at the t's in what I hope is an annoying manner. She has no right not to sound more North American. That fact somehow over-rides the contrition her voice should no doubt evoke. "My perspective," I continue, "is this." And here I deliver the goods, as best I can. Emily is an enigma to me, as she always has been. Though I love her dearly, goes without saying. What she wants, who knows? She has no job but spends much of her time preparing to look for one. Seems to have a lot of friends, some from the old days, some newly acquired. Extremely active social life, despite the absence of income. Leaves me in charge of my, our grandchildren a lot, both well by the way. The situation in a nutshell.

"What of that oaf Terry Foley? Emily told me he's been lurking about."

"He sort of hangs around. She's refusing to have anything to do with him. But of course he must have the right to see the kids. I expect to be caught in the middle for some time to come."

"Better you than me." One of the things Sandra and I agreed about in the aftermath of the breakup was the horrific miscasting of Terry Foley in the role of Emily's boyfriend. But in the brief pause that follows, I realize that I've been visualizing Sandra not as she must be now, the greying grandma of Emily's photos, fastened (as of course I am) to a dying animal, but as though she's calling from our first apartment in Vancouver, calling from three decades back, perhaps the month Emily was conceived. The twenty-seven-year-old Sandra – younger than Emily is now! – speaking words that have nothing to do with the banality of the current instant, words that cut to the heart's chase.

Words about what?

Innocence. The word – when was the last time I used it? – manifests itself in some twilight zone of my attention. Our coming together inspired, instigated by her innocence, my perception of, perspective on, her innocence.

But the contemporary Sandra is continuing to talk. I miss the first part of her sentence.

"… a bit concerned. Especially after that business with that last woman, I've forgotten her name? You know how you tend to lose your bearings when things go wonky. There's a question of your, well, stability."

This is the same old Sandra, complete honesty,

complete absence of tact. What I have to keep in mind is that, appearances to the contrary, she's not trying to insult me, she's really not. But "wonky"? Give me a break.

And what does she know about "that last woman" anyway? Wasn't that at least two years ago?

"Do I not sound reasonably stable?"

"Oh you *sound* stable," she says, as though a video or perhaps an X-ray might reveal something else altogether.

"Well, why wouldn't I be 'stable,' as you put it, then?"

"I only mean, a man of your age must feel somewhat disoriented after–"

"A man of *my* age, which is also *your* age."

"Yes, but our circumstances are very different."

She's referring to her airtight second marriage, to a widower named Keith, over whom, according to Emily, she towers. And I have to hand it to her, reinventing herself at forty-plus after I dumped her, moving to Ontario, going back to school, entering a new profession, and, most miraculous of all, managing to conjure up Keith, wiry little Keith, as Emily refers to him.

Perhaps I have idealized Sandra, patron saint of un-pettiness. Gliding through the lower depths, I see the colourful insect flit enticingly overhead, but damned if I'm going to snap at it.

"Yes, they are quite different. I am, however, not disoriented. Though I do appreciate your concern."

She's been talking at the same time. "… eccentric, irrational streak that might resurface at a time like this, with all the stress of Emily and the children descending on you. To say nothing of Foley's being added to the mix."

"There is a certain amount of stress, yes. But I can handle it." Keep those teeth clenched, Norman.

"You used not to be so adept at handling stress."

I'm determined not to lose it here, for the sake of that voice from 1971.

"I am aware of my deficiencies in the area of stress-handling. I've been striving to overcome them. I believe I'm succeeding."

This is the woman who at twenty-seven had had only one lover before me, who pronounced the middle "e" in veg-e-table, who was twenty-one and at Oxford before she had ever heard anyone say the word "fuck" (an upper-crusty girl who'd dropped an armload of books), who after graduating had come with her friend Charlotte to teach in northern BC, commenting as she called the roll on the first day, the class list an anthology of Koslowskis and Kowalchuks, "What funny names." She and Charlotte watching *Hockey Night in Canada* because there was absolutely no other thinkable Saturday night alternative. Confessing embarrassing (to me), but not embarrassed, puzzlement in a UBC grad seminar when the word "Om" cropped up, the lone member of her generation not to be a Zen master. Professing her body incapable of lovemaking after 8 p.m. Speaking truth always, without regard for consequences. Solemnly offering me this bizarre package of what I now call innocence, which I patronizingly accepted, and fed off for however many years, to my unacknowledged shame. She has the right to say anything she pleases about me and stress.

Charlotte, her real soul-mate, had the sense to glom onto a cheerful dumbass Doukhobor schoolteacher with a God-given ability to acquire lucrative rental properties in Surrey. Sandra drew the short straw.

"Well!" she's saying now. "I won't labour the point. You do sound a bit upset just now."

And this of course is what did us in, this relentlessness combined with, ultimately, my boredom with her innocence, her obstinate failure to become other than what she'd always been, perfect material for a low-budget remake of an Updike story about marriage, one in which the cheated-on wife refuses to recognize what's happening, her version of the world hermetically separated from the adult reality of flux and passion. Yet I envied her that innocence, wanted some for myself, some but not all, impossible in more than one sense.

The conversation ends, Sandra struggling to close on a positive note – "I'm glad you're, um, still in good health" – and I sink back to 1971, perfect sunny October in Vancouver, Rod Stewart endlessly bellowing "Wake up Maggie, I think I got something to say to you," Sandra on the phone the morning after we first nearly fucked – "I think I behaved badly and so did you" – probably the only lie she ever told me, no, not a lie – initial bargaining position would be more charitable and accurate. Remembering the stray hair sprouting shamelessly from her left aureole, destined soon to disappear forever. Days later the young in one another's arms, fingers reverently fondling each other's genitalia as Sandra pronounced her blue-eyed judgment, as though somewhere notes were being taken: "It's good to lie like this."

Chapter Five

I arrive at the coffee place precisely on time, but Raissa McCloskey is nowhere to be seen. This is not unexpected. She likes to make entrances. Today the audience, in addition to me, consists of a gaggle of young women, and two or three young men. Young is the key word here. I sense cool gazes being directed my way, then quickly shifted elsewhere; no doubt I've been categorized as an elderly aberration.

I'm not used to drinking coffee from a vessel cosseted by a cardboard sleeve.

The women seem younger than my first-year students. They have super-straight hair, ironically besloganed tee-shirts, and low-cut jeans. The young man closest to me is tall, with a neatly trimmed beard and flat belly, and what appears to me to be a carefully cultivated "serious" demeanour. He would surely have to be called (for example) David not Dave. I fear that if we make eye contact, he'll want to get my opinion on a manuscript of poems with titles like "We're All Beothuks Now" or on a grant application for a project involving the erection of inflatable Picasso-inspired whales in unlikely public places. A small satchel leans menacingly against a leg of his chair.

I sip uneasily.

If "dervish" were a verb, that would be how Raissa comes in. Effulgent halo of red hair, her clothing a flash of pink, white, and baby blue, a hand placed briefly against her forehead as though shading her eyes from an imaginary sun, Cortez-like on the peak in Darien. And me, for an instant, as she smiles, the vast Pacific. Despite myself, I'm flattered.

According to Emily, most of the men who know Raissa are in love with her, at least in Raissa's own estimation. Fortunately for everyone, she's happily married, as they say, a fact – once more according to Emily – she tends to announce rather frequently, some-times brandishing her wedding ring like a fragment of the true cross.

But that's not the bottom line on Raissa. Unlike most of the David-not-Daves, she has real talent, and it's been recognized. Her half-hour film, *Speaking in Tongues*, has won several national awards. The storyline features a young woman inexplicably stranded in St. John's. She makes attempts to communicate using an incompre-hensible made-up language. She's able to make known her need for food and shelter, but nothing beyond that. In a number of brief scenes she encounters uncomprehending and unsympathetic people in the downtown, a sad world of drizzle and mist, her frustration increasing by the frame. These scenes are counterpointed by short animation sequences indicating that she believes she comes from some fairytale kingdom of castles and pastoral landscapes.

The St. John's of the film is reminiscent of the world of the early Truffaut, *Shoot the Piano Player*, for example.

In fact there's a curious resonance between the young woman and the Charles Aznavour character, the same sort of pathos and comedy generated by her plight. Finally she meets a young man who somehow manages to intuit what she wants. Together they drive to a community around the bay. She leads him to a sunlit headland, where she shows him a wooden structure covered with golden origami birds. At her urging he picks up one of them, and it comes to life, taking flight into a sky which evolves into the animated world of her imagination, gradually filling the screen as the film ends.

In context, it's – believe it or not – not sentimental. There's a lightness of touch that suggests the filmmaker herself is aware of the kitschiness of her artificial paradise and invites the viewer to share her amusement but also to see it as a metaphor for something more serious.

"Here," Raissa says, producing a newspaper clipping and thrusting it at me. "She left this on my kitchen table yesterday."

But it's impossible not to look at Raissa as she marches off to order her beverage. Everybody but David checks her out.

The article is short, from a Vancouver newspaper. It describes an apparently deliberate hit-and-run involving a man struck by a car driven by a woman, witnessed by a number of bystanders, some of whom had also noticed the driver conversing with a second woman in a supermarket parking lot shortly before the event. The victim was reported to be in critical condition. Police were looking for the driver and the woman to whom she had been speaking. No one had taken note of the licence number, and witness accounts of the car's make and model were inconsistent. Descriptions of the women were equally unhelpful. Both wore sunglasses, for example. Police were appealing to the public for information. The man's identity was being withheld.

Raissa returns with her coffee.

"She's one of those women." She's daring me to disagree. I foresee the banality of the ensuing dialogue if I do.

"Which one?"

"I don't know. Does it matter?"

It comes to me immediately that Raissa is lying, that she knows the truth, the whole truth, and that the entire operation with its ridiculous cloak-and-daggerness is designed to soften me up, to cushion the blow.

"So you think Emily is capable of being the driver in a deliberate hit-and-run?"

Raissa feigns thoughtfulness, I think, as she gazes into the middle distance for a moment. "Yes," she says rather too decisively. She makes a sweeping gesture that seems to jolt David out of his reverie. "Any of us, given the right circumstances …"

"Bullshit, Raissa." It's David, suddenly looming over our table, staring down, it seems from my angle, at Raissa's breasts, sliver of cleavage only from where I sit – perhaps the view from up there is more rewarding. Apparently he's been eavesdropping-not-daydreaming. He looks familiar now, too. But that's a common experience around here. "You yourself, Raissa, would not be capable of running someone down. I wouldn't, either. Nor, I suspect, would this gentleman. The all-too-easy assumption that–"

Raissa, unsurprised, manages to cut him off by

raising her voice only slightly. "Aaron, why are you such an asshole?"

Aaron-not-David interrupts himself, pauses as if to give Raissa's query the serious consideration it deserves, then decides that laughing it off is the best response. He chuckles with forced heartiness. "That's a pretty big why, Raissa."

As he says this I recognize him as the male lead in *Speaking in Tongues.* Raissa introduces us, somewhat resignedly. He announces that he must be on his way but it was nice meeting me and he'll be seeing Raissa around, a remark which causes her to wince, or, more probably, causes her to simulate wincing.

As soon as he's out the door, she leans over towards me. "Between you and I? I think he's stalking me."

I point out that he was here swilling his latte before she arrived. She dismisses this with a hand motion that indicates what I've said is too trivial to rebut. "Several people knew I was coming."

Including Emily, I'd bet, but I don't say anything.

"He's been sort of infatuated with me since the film. I was hoping if I ignored him today, he'd leave me alone and that'd be a sign he's got over it."

"In any case," I say, trying to get us back on track, "I sort of agree with him. *You* wouldn't drive into someone on purpose. Nor would Emily. Plus, I think you know more than you're letting on."

She ignores this last comment. "So you think she's the other one."

"I don't necessarily think she's either one." To my surprise, I'm starting to feel an irritation that could blossom into anger any minute now. My daughter has committed or abetted a serious crime; she can't bring herself to tell me about it but wants me to know; nor can she tell her friend directly but instead leaves a newspaper clipping describing the crime on the friend's kitchen table, certain that the friend, known not to be the soul of discretion, will convey this intelligence to me. Or: she and her friend together cook up the last part as a way of breaking it to me gently. Either way I'm being played, conned. Clearly in the category of "beneath my dignity."

Raissa has caught the proto-hostility in my tone. "Well," she says, flicking her hand, palm up, at the clipping, "I've done my duty."

Duty to whom? I wonder. Emily? Me? Herself, more likely. To her sense of who she is. Whatever that means to her now. She's an artist, wife, mother, in who knows which order. I think briefly of who she was ten years ago, in my creative writing class, reading a poem describing the speaker's liberating experience of throwing a history textbook into the air, in context an exuberant repudiation of the constraints of the past. A self-satisfied little smile as she finished it. Take that, history. So much for you, convention, custom, all wearisomely didactic blasts from the past. We're talking present tense now, all things made new.

She was about twenty then. And I feel my own little smile forming as I think that she probably wouldn't write that poem now.

"What?" she says, suspicious but friendlier, now that I'm not going to explode.

She listens patiently while I explain and then tells me that she has no memory of that particular poem.

In the last section of *Isle of the Blessed*, things unravel quickly. The monk has grown old. The fish are no longer abundant. At the monk's suggestion, a form of rationing is adopted, something never before known on the island. So enamoured are the islanders of their leisure activities that they scarcely notice this change. Eating less means nothing to them. What is important is engaging in self-consciously "balanced" behaviour – and in applying the increasingly complicated and sophisticated rules for evaluating it.

Then something unexpected happens. A humble young woman from the remotest peninsula claims to have visions. At least this is how the monk interprets the news. The islanders of course have no word for "vision." The phrase that the young woman uses is "visiting the world inside my head." A charismatic figure, she attracts large crowds wherever she goes. Her message is that the world inside one's head is as real as the world of daily experience. She speaks, the monk hears, with such conviction that many come to believe her, and concomitantly, to question the now-established norms of their society.

Incredibly, since there is no island tradition of such things, she begins to attack the monk in her speeches. The "monk's game" had blinded her audiences to the existence of the inner world, the world which is, she says, the source of the islanders' being – a notion which, ironically, could not have been articulated before the monk's arrival – and also the source of the wisdom which inspired them to fish in the old way, when just the right amount was harvested annually. There are reports that many of her listeners actually experience hunger pangs at this point in her orations, as though (as the monk puts it) "she was breaking the spell I had cast on her compatriots – or was casting a new one herself."

"The monk's game is a lie which is destroying us," she shouts in conclusion. "Look inside yourselves and discover the truth."

The monk can't resist going, incognito, to see for himself. He hovers on the periphery of the crowd. But as fate would have it, just as the young woman's rhetoric is building to its climax, a small boy standing nearby recognizes him, cries out, and his identity is revealed.

"I am seized by the mob, like so many before me," he says in the novel's last paragraph. "I see in their faces the primal ignorance I set out to eradicate. But as I taste death at their hands, I will content myself with the knowledge that, without me, they would be incapable of so imaginative an act."

The echo of the ending of *L'Étranger*, groaningly obvious to me, will come as front-page news to the hypothetical readers of *Contemporary Canadian Novelists*. Beyond that, what can one say? That the ending is "ironic." That the understanding of life implied by the novel as a whole is mean-spirited and cynical. That the smartass narrative voice both intrigues me and pisses me off. That last one will have to be modified somewhat, a task for another day.

Late afternoon, time for my run. I park by the lake, next to the cemetery, hop out, and start chugging. Within a minute or two I have a companion: Rupert Stiggins, renowned distance runner and departmental pariah. He peers at me with what I take to be condescension, as if to say, My whippet-like body is far superior to yours, but it's admirable that, ungainly as yours is, you haven't given up entirely.

"Cheers," he says. "Mind a bit of company?" It's not really a question.

"Rupert, I don't think I can keep up with you."

"No problem. I'll slow down to your pace."

"And I can't really converse while I'm running."

"No problem there, either," Rupert says genially, clearly prepared to treat me to a monologue. This has happened two or three times before. I recognize that there's no way out.

Perhaps there's a Rupert in every English department: the one colleague who gets along with almost no one, the one colleague against whom everyone else, despite their bitter differences with each other, can unite and declare, as with one voice: this man is an asshole. It's taken Rupert years to achieve this status, and it's all the more impressive that he's done it not by committing large public gaffes but rather by offending everyone individually in pointlessly petty ways. Anecdotes abound about his miserly punctiliousness with respect to small sums of money, his tendency to make denigrating remarks about other people's scholarly achievements, his gratuitous withholding of minor courtesies, his general obstinacy.

Yet I've somehow managed to stay on speaking terms with him. For some reason we've never found ourselves at odds. We exchange pleasantries and move on, unless he decides I've given him licence to complain about something. I can't bring myself to be rude to him, perhaps, it's occurred to me, because his North of England accent reminds me in a distant way of Sandra's.

His monologue begins as soon as we start moving. It lasts for the entire circuit of the lake, with longish pauses from time to time, during which I make the occasional non-committal grunt as a sign that I have, in fact, been paying attention.

"… dispute with the city of St. John's regarding the assessed value of my house … dispute with the next door neighbours, the Brownes. Brownes with an 'e,' mind you. The ordinary way would not be good enough for them. Regarding the leakage of my roof, which, as a qualified third-party opinion has established, is directly attributable to problems with their roof. Our dwellings being physically adjoined, and their roof, as my misfortune would have it, being slightly higher than mine.

"… contacted my insurance company. In due course they dispatched a person with some expertise in roofing. He quickly determined that the fault indeed lay with their structure and not mine. He and I separately made phone calls to the Browne residence, leaving numerous messages, never receiving the courtesy of a reply …"

There follows a digression on the state of the Brownes' marriage, on the brink of dissolution, Rupert believes, Desmond Browne having moved to Toronto some months back, ostensibly for professional reasons.

I'm gasping as I try to maintain a respectable "slow" pace for Rupert, while he chatters non-stop, probably not having broken a sweat, his long hairless legs moving in effortless mockery of my own choppy strides.

"… managed to obtain Desmond's e-mail address. I sent him a reasoned and dispassionate account of the situation. Shortly thereafter receiving a lengthy reply, remarkable for its vitriolic tone and content. Hinting none too subtly that since his sister is a lawyer, the Brownes would have access to unlimited free legal advice should the occasion arise ..."

At approximately this point my attention wanders. I've tried hard to pay close attention in case he asks my opinion of something at the end of it all, but enough is enough.

"... bedroom wall adjoining the Brownes' house continues to slobber on cue after each substantial rain ..."

We're well over the halfway mark now, making pretty good time too, though out of misplaced courtesy I haven't been checking my watch obsessively, as I normally would. I tune out completely until we're almost finished.

"... carefully worded letters to the appropriate bureaucrats which have, without exception, gone un-answered. Reasoned requests for civilized dialogue ..."

"Here we are, Rupert."

He looks puzzled. "You're doing only the one lap, are you? See you later then." Exit Rupert, thank God.

The signature Rupert anecdote flits through my mind. Forced by an odd set of social circumstances to stand the chronically impecunious Bill Duffett a pint at a departmental function, Rupert shortly thereafter sends Duffett, via internal mail, a Canadian Tire flyer advertising, among much else, some small item whose price was circled in red marker. Attached was a note reading in part, "... I am as you know without transport and therefore unable to take advantage of this excellent price, which corresponds almost exactly to the cost of the pint of beer that I recently bought you." (And why was he "without transport"? Because he's too cheap to buy a car.)

On the drive home, Rupert and Emily compete for the role of object of my contemplation. An unlikely pairing, Stiggins the departmental scapegoat, loved by none, reviled – behind his back – by almost all. Does he know this? Or is the collective personality of our colleagues as much an enigma to him as Emily has become to me?

And have I become, for Emily, some version of Stiggins, someone who has assumed the exaggerated dimensions of the Other and who therefore cannot be construed as human, let alone an ally? Let alone someone who fancies himself a source of unconditional love.

For the real mystery here is not what Emily did or didn't do in Vancouver, but rather why we can't even talk directly about it. Just as no one will ever tell Stiggins to his face that he's an asshole, so a ritual politeness permeates my interaction with Emily. True, her marriage has not been the occasion for wholehearted parental joy, and she has been well aware of this, but no one attempted to prevent its occurrence, and no one – except possibly Sandra – is now saying I told you so.

Would it have killed me to let her move in back when? But why would that rejection have been the catalyst for the decade-long Little Ice Age? There's no telling.

On cue, the Basilica looms judgmentally into my field of vision. Okay, okay, it's all my fault. But how can I make amends, other than by welcoming her into my, our home? Which I've already done.

Another dad might storm into the house, brandishing the clipping, demanding enlightenment. But he would have no clue what he would be up against: Samantha screaming about some injustice involving toys, Ryan explaining the intricacies of a computer game to the bemused Dobrila and Sunila, who, ignoring his chatter as best they can, converse in one of their languages that is not English, in the background the radio perpetually tuned to the CBC, the *Fisheries Broadcast* guy saying something about the skate fishery in 3PS. And in the middle of it all, monosyllabic, poker-faced, an adult daughter seasoned in the techniques of plausible deniability.

Ryan's team goes through its warm-ups, the only time he'll ever have a chance to score a goal, or get a shot for that matter. The boys line up in single file, the ball placed indecently close to the net. Ryan does a couple of false starts, then runs and drives the ball along the ground directly at the keeper, who scoops it up nonchalantly. He then ambles to the back of the line, unconcerned, as a more competent teammate takes two short steps and hammers the ball into the upper right corner of the net.

When the game starts I count the number of times Ryan touches the ball. This has become a bit of a bond between us; he likes to know that I'm keeping tabs on his every move. Everything counts, on the principle that even inadvertent contact means he's somewhere close to the centre of the action. The game is played in eight five-minute shifts, two of which, if the team has a normal complement of players, he will sit out. When he comes to the sideline I keep him posted on his totals – twenty is a reasonable target for a game – as I hand him his water bottle.

And then it happens, the disaster I've been, I suddenly realize, waiting for. The crisis. The moment when one proves one's mettle as a grandfather. Ryan is running toward me, face bloodied, screaming. Why wasn't I looking? (Okay, it was the thirtyish mom in her folding chair maybe ten yards down the sideline, with her – relatively, relatively – skimpy top.)

In any case, now it's battle stations. It's hard to tell what the problem is, and how serious. "He's not good with pain," Emily has told me. "A wuss, like his father." The coach, seeing that Ryan has spotted me, concludes that nothing further is required of him and motions for a substitute to get onto the field. No parent comes over to offer assistance. Perhaps this is my payback for my failure to engage in chitchat with them, or perhaps it's merely assumed that I'll be as competent as they would be with their own kids.

Ryan shoves his face at me, sobbing. There's blood around his mouth, but not that much. I wipe it away with my handkerchief, trying to convince him and myself that I know what I'm doing. The blood seems to be coming from a small cut on his upper lip. But as I look into his mouth, something else seems amiss. There's a stubby white protrusion jutting up from the gumline of his lower jaw. A foreign object? Or could a tooth have broken off? It takes several seconds for me to realize that it's a brand new tooth surfacing.

He's calmed down a bit now, perhaps distracted by

the attention I've been paying to his mouth instead of his lip. I tell him the cut is tiny, and no longer bleeding. "Do you want to go home?"

"No."

I haven't been expecting anything so definite. "Do you want to keep playing?"

A vigorous nod.

I signal to the coach, who wanders up and down the field, following the play.

"He's ready." With what bizarrely misplaced pride do I utter the foregoing.

The coach looks briefly at Ryan. "Next shift," he says. At the end of the game I tell Ryan he's had twenty-two touches. And most were intentional. He smiles, almost indulgently, mind elsewhere.

On the way home, I ponder the clichéd nature of the evening's experience, the juxtaposition of the injury with the discovery of the tooth. I'd like to explain to Ryan the poignant irony of the situation: the tooth driving upward through the flesh, exemplum of growth, harbinger of potency; the bloodied lip, emblem of vulnerability, mortality even. His own reflexive courage in plunging back into the fray, yadda yadda yadda.

What I say is, "So you've got a new tooth coming in. That's exciting, hey?"

"Yeah. Not as exciting as losing one, though. The tooth fairy brings me five dollars."

"Five dollars a tooth?" Another sign of my out-of-touchness.

"Some kids get more." He says this without rancour.

"And some get less?"

"I guess so."

This wearisome message about economic inequality has been brought to you by: Granddad. I can't think of anything more to say.

We pull into the driveway. "Thank you for taking me to soccer," he says. There's something disquieting about his constant politeness, which echoes Emily's – engaging on the surface, but also a distancing device. I've heard him say "I love you" to Emily in precisely the tone he's just used, not nakedly political but somehow perfunctory, boilerplate.

All of which seems, sadly, a reflection of Emily and me.

I am, I realize, as Ryan's cleats scrape on the front walk, afraid of my daughter. Afraid of what I believe her to be, and perhaps more afraid that she has mutated into someone who would, against all odds based on past performance, at the moment of confrontation blurt angry, tear-punctuated truths, a left hook out of nowhere sending me down for the count. Better the daughter you know. Perhaps.

Suppertime is uneventful. I give a slightly exaggerated account of Ryan's bravery on the soccer pitch. The tooth is, of course, no news to Emily. She seems a bit skeptical about Ryan's desire to get back into the game but doesn't pursue the issue.

She gives no sign that Raissa has told her about our meeting. After she has gone to bed (why always so early? exhaustion? depression?), I decide to leave the clipping on the kitchen table. I know that this is cowardly and that I will pay for it, big-time.

Then I decide not to do it after all.

Chapter Six

Morning. A day at the university looms. First a department meeting to deal with the upcoming external review. Next, various bits of busywork in preparation for the upcoming semester. A former student needs a letter of reference sent out pronto. Mid-afternoon, there's my fortnightly date with Bill Duffett for a beer or three at the student pub.

It's only eight-thirty, but Emily already has the kids breakfasting efficiently. This is a bit unusual, as she often leaves that chore to Sunila (and now Dobrila), due to arrive at nine. But they have the day off, Emily tells me, as she's arranged to take the kids on an outing somewhere with her friend Daphne Willicott, whose daughter is about Samantha's age. Daphne will pick them up around ten.

I listen carefully for signs that Raissa has told her that she's told me, though what those signs would be is a good question.

"We'll probably go to Topsail Beach," she's saying, "back late afternoon at the earliest. We'll probably have supper at Daphne's."

The meeting is held in a regular classroom, one of many whose acoustics seems designed to prevent communication. From time to time a noise resembling that of a vacuum cleaner erupts, as if to reinforce the institutional verity that, bad as things are, they can always get worse.

The Vice-President (Academic) looks like a Boy Scout. He has a shiny forehead and horn-rimmed glasses. His hair seems to have no discernible colour. He speaks in a monotone which would, even under ordinary circumstances, be barely audible. He's saying something, I think, about the need for the department to redefine itself, how the external review should be understood as an opportunity, not something to be feared, a chance for us to set our course – I'm assuming it *was* "set your course" not "wet your horse" – for the next ten years.

I glance around at my colleagues, ensconced in the semi-circle of desks that Greg Harkness, the department head, has insisted on in his introductory comments. The seating arrangement will, he said, "enhance collegiality," a phrase delivered in such a way that we can construe irony or not; it's up to us. It's as if he has mentally divided the department into two groups, the hip and the clueless. Every public statement he makes can be interpreted by each group according to its own lights. And he can always claim, when pressed, that he "really meant" or "didn't really mean" what he's said. In such wise he has governed the department without major mishap – or innovation – for three years now. But for whatever reason, he's now had enough, and hence the soon-to-be-resolved Plover vs. Pike contest.

About fifteen of us have shown up, around half the department's regular faculty, a large turnout given the time of year. I've no idea what this means. People are worried? People are looking for opportunities to advance their individual "agendas"? More likely, we're here partly out of a sense of duty, partly out of a hope-against-hope that someone will make a fool of him/herself. Who knows? They're an inscrutable lot, my colleagues, when it comes to matters of general professional concern.

And few of us will be around in ten years. I register with a combination of malice and sadness the pro-liferation of saggy jowls, veined calves, thickened torsos, balding pates. Collectively we have no interest in wetting our horse in any direction. Someone has pulled the plug; as a department we're content to spin around for a while before the inevitable presents itself. Our median age is mine, fifty-eight. We have one recently hired *wunderkind* of thirty. After that, our youngest is forty-six, the perpetually and often exasperatingly boyish Nathan Grainger.

And even Grainger, I realize, used to have a lot more hair.

Tonight I'll be seeing Maureen Finnerty. Tonight will be the night, maybe. Should be. Her poetry not an issue, now a source of playful jest. Terms and conditions to be tacitly negotiated, both of us wary of overt declarations of this or that, but understandings will be arrived at. Sealed with a kiss, and more. Or so I dream.

Barney Power, at the desk beside me, nudges a piece of paper in my direction. On it he has written:

Anglo-Irishman: a Protestant on a horse. He leans over and whispers, "Brendan Behan." There need be no context for this sort of thing, as far as Barney is concerned. Since he established, early on, that I'm not an anglophile, he's assumed that I'm the perfect audience for Brit-bashing, ready to gratify him with a belly-laugh or, if circumstances prevent that, a conspiratorial smile, which I'm pleased to provide him with now. (Has he, too, heard "horse" instead of "course"?)

To avoid engaging in whispery dialogue with Barney, I direct my attention to the front of the room where the Boy Scout continues to hold forth. Relatively new in his role as VP (Academic), a philosopher in a previous existence, he exudes the aura of failed self-importance that characterized those of his predecessors that I can remember. One, a scion of what was once Newfoundland's ruling class, was fond of comparing the operation of the university to that of a fish-plant. Another, an exotic import, insisted that we speak officially in terms of "clients" instead of "students," and "delivering pedagogical services" rather than "teaching." It's too early to get a handle on this one, though the smart money thinks he's presenting symptoms of anal-retentive bean-counting. Which would be bad news for the Faculty of Arts. But then almost any news is.

The veep has come with a retinue. There's a secretary whose function is to nod emphatically at everything he says. There are two faculty members, unknown to me, from units that have recently been reviewed. One is a woman from Fine Arts who looks like something out of Dürer, blocky Germanic face, black bangs, something ascetic in her demeanour. She might be in her mid-forties, distinctly unpretty, but who knows what's under the dark blue button-up-the-front skirt. Dark, thick-looking stockings prevent direct viewing of the legs. Clunky black sandally things on her feet. The upper regions of the body cloaked in a shapeless sweater. Unknowable. Enigmatic.

And now she's speaking! With the conviction of a newly minted Moonie, she extols the virtues of having undergone a review. I lose interest in her immediately. Then the other faculty member speaks. He looks a bit like D. H. Lawrence in the photo that used to appear on the back cover of the Penguin edition of *Sons and Lovers* and the others. But he's from engineering. The external review was good for them, too, I think he's saying, especially helpful in pinpointing their hierarchy of priorities for the next decade.

When it's over, and we're all shuffling out into the corridor, Eddie Laskowski asks, of no one in particular, and not too loudly, "What sort of philosopher becomes an administrator?" He waits a few seconds, then gives the answer: "A cynic."

Back in my office not five minutes and there's a knock on the door. Brian Henighan, most distinctive student ever to enter a classroom of mine. The fourth-year Romantics seminar, two years ago: Henighan, having been out of school for some years, needed the course in order to get into the Education Faculty as someone who could, at a pinch, teach English, though his real professional ambition was to teach phys ed. He was about thirty, understatedly athletic in physique and movements, somehow conveying the sense that he could, if required, make his body perform in ways most of us would find impossible. Later I learned that he was a well-known local marathoner and had played on the provincial soccer team in more than one national tournament.

In any case, Henighan the Romanticist. At once it became evident that he was (a) unusually, naively keen, and (b) assiduous in finding Christian references everywhere, usually involving the Virgin Mary. None of this endeared him to his younger classmates, whose rolling eyes and half-heartedly concealed smirks quickly began to accompany his increasingly complex analyses. This reaction of course pissed me off. What instructor is pleased with undergraduate displays of amusedly world-weary superiority, however passively manifested? I would, in revenge, egg Brian on. Yes, perhaps conventional scholarship had been behind the eight-ball in failing to identify the female figure in "The Mental Traveller" as the Virgin Mary. Yes, while Coleridge was no Roman Catholic, it was indeed possible that both the mariner and the poet himself could say, "To Mary Queen the praise be given!" in a straightforward, non-ironic way. Who in the class would care to refute such an approach? At such moments no one would, in fact, care to look up from his or her text, let alone open his or her mouth. How uncool of me to suggest such a possibility.

As the semester went on, I encouraged Brian to stray farther and farther from the course syllabus in what, it became clear, was a low-key, good-natured attempt to proselytize. Yes, Brian, feel free to read that rather fulsome passage from Chesterton that you think is relevant to what Wordsworth is saying here. Yes, do read out that letter from Tolkien to his son that seems actually to have nothing at all to do with the course – one in which Tolkien said (I'm paraphrasing) that he loved mass best of all when it was said by a backward country priest in front of a congregation of rustic ignoramuses, that there was something purer and more authentic about receiving the Blessed Sacrament under those conditions.

He started coming around during my office hours. As in some parody of *The Exorcist*, it began to seem that the real target of his waging of spiritual warfare was not the callow *lumpenmass* of his fellow students, but me, the secular priest whose soul would be the real prize. He plied me with books, Evelyn Waugh's biography of Thomas Campion, for example, which I read at one sitting. I especially savoured Waugh's line that in order to believe in the spiritual legitimacy of Anglicanism, one would have to think that God revealed His will to a particular group of Englishmen who, in the process of responding to it, just happened to be in line to gain financially in a big way.

I could picture Brian, ascetic-seeming as he was, as one of the group of young men studying to be priests on the Continent, preparing to infiltrate their native land like so many Romish jihadists – though of course two years ago I didn't know that last word. I could see Brian moving clandestinely from one country house to the next, hearing confessions, saying mass for masters and servants alike, hiding in the priest-holes, the chaste intimacy of the women's assistance in tending to his creaturely needs, the endless risk to all concerned, the secret blossoming of grace in the soul of a stable boy, unknown, alas, to Father Brian, master of disguise, who has already passed on to the next estate like the Mariner himself, his strange power of speech manifesting itself in incomprehensible Latin around yet another makeshift altar.

Or so my Romantic vision of Brian went. In truth he was no priest, though he would have liked to be one, he confided, but he was a married man, two children, toddlers, the second autistic, no thought – of course, it hardly needed to be spoken – of contraception. Yes, he knew how it sounded, but he and his wife had learned to trust the Lord, and there had been one occasion when, in answer to prayer, a significant amount of cash had turned up in their apartment mailbox. He'd paused when he said this, as though giving me room and even licence to scoff if I chose. It turned out that the source of the money was another member of his Marian-oriented prayer group, in turn trusting his Spirit-inspired impulse. I could believe it or not, as I chose.

He disliked his other English course, he told me, the Modern Poetry one in which he'd been forced to study Ted Hughes and Sylvia Plath. "There's so much spiritual darkness in their work." What could I do but agree? There *is* spiritual darkness in their work. "But we're supposed to *like* the darkness," he said. "We're supposed to pretend there's something profound about it, when it's only self-indulgence." No argument from me. What was startling was that someone taking courses cared about such questions.

Once I used the word "infusion" in class, and he came around to tell me that "infusion" had a quite particular theological meaning of which he wasn't sure I was aware. I reminded him that many words are coined as technical terms but gradually acquire broader, more flexible, more popular meanings. "That's what I don't like about language," he said. "Words should mean one thing and one thing only. Meanings shouldn't be allowed to change."

Another time he told me that despite how he might seem then, he'd led a pretty wild life up until about five years ago – unholy living, sinful relationships, even a brush or two with the law. And before that, as an altar boy, he'd been abused over a period of years by a diocesan priest, not one of the big name ones, if that's what I was thinking, but one who'd never been caught. "But I came through all that," he said. "And I forgive him."

And in the end there had been no invitation to come along to a meeting, no challenge to try things on or check things out, the logical next step in what I'd supposed to be his campaign to win me over – only a respectful handshake and a kind comment or two about the course.

This condensed history of Brian Henighan is what flashes through my mind in the several seconds after I recognize him, as, smiling, I extend my hand.

"Dr. Norman," he says. "How are you?"

The voice reminds me that what I like about Brian is the absence of any aura of nuttiness of the sort one might construe to lie behind the facts outlined above. He's not that stock figure of pop culture, the religious fanatic who's ready to "snap" or "explode." Instead he gives the impression of balance and sanity in a way that, for example, few of my colleagues are able to manage.

"Fine," I say, perhaps too perfunctorily. He peers

into my eyes an instant longer than socially mandated. He once told me that he had the gift of discernment. Perhaps he thinks I should confess.

Why is he here? He's been "led," he tells me. He and his wife were driving along Elizabeth Avenue when he realized that he hadn't seen me in two years and this would be a good time to drop in. Though he often drives along Elizabeth, this was the first time that making contact had occurred to him.

"And your wife?"

"Waiting in the car. I can't stay long."

He passes a business card to me. He works for an insurance company whose offices are in Churchill Square, he explains. He realized last year that he'd need to get a job, fast – "the third one was on the way" – and this seemed to be his best bet. He'd spent a couple of months training in Halifax, in a place that, as he described it, sounded somehow monastic – separated from his family, the days devoted to learning the ropes of the insurance business in some combination of solitary study and communal instruction. There's something wistful in his tone, though he acknowledges the hardship that his wife experienced during his absence.

Insurance is a good career choice, he says, because it allows him to help people. Though it's hard, really hard, to make sales. He's not a closer. He doesn't want to pry, but how am I fixed for life insurance? He doesn't wait for an answer. No pressure, but if I have a few dollars to invest, he can give me a better rate on a GIC than I can get anywhere else. But that's not really why he's come.

He reaches into his briefcase, pulls out a video cassette. "I think you'll be interested in this. Maybe we can have coffee sometime, once you've had a chance to look at it. It's called *Mary's Miraculous Medal*. I know you're interested in things like this. It only runs for half an hour. I'd like to know what you think."

"Okay, I'll look at it for sure. Soon."

"And one more thing." This time he reaches into a pocket, withdraws a small leather pouch, extricates a tiny oval piece of metal, perhaps three-quarters of an inch long. "This was blessed. At Medjugorge." I must look blank. "You know, the place in Yugoslavia or what used to be Yugoslavia where the Blessed Virgin has appeared to some children? I got to go there last year." He can afford to do that? "A friend in our prayer group put up the money," he says, reading my mind, or face. "It's most efficacious if you wear it next to the skin. I really have to go now. But I'll be in touch." He says this as he presses the sanctified object into my palm. "I know you'll take this seriously. It ties in with the tape." He's gone before I can look at what he's given me.

It's a medal with the image of the Virgin on the front, encircled by a Latin motto: *Regine since labe originali concepta OPN*, with a date, 1830, at the bottom.

I remember Brian's telling me that he had once consulted a lawyer about the possibility of suing a certain philosophy professor for making blasphemous comments in class. It would, the lawyer told him, be a waste of money.

Later, beer with Bill Duffett in the almost empty student pub.

It began, Duffett says, with phone calls to his house. The first two times, one of the kids answered. They reported hearing a female voice speaking incoherently in a Chinese accent. It was difficult for them to discern individual words. It was never clear what the woman wanted. Attempts to engage her in dialogue resulted only in further incoherence. And the voice was somehow feeble, close to inaudible. They would routinely hang up after a minute or so.

Then Duffett himself happened to answer the third call. There was something familiar about the voice. When Duffett identified himself, she responded with what would have seemed like excitement, if she had been able to speak louder. Who are you? Duffett found himself shouting.

Finally she gave him a name he recognized, a woman from the PRC who'd been his student in two language courses in the early nineties. She'd been doing a master's degree in linguistics, and Duffett's cross-listed offerings were part of her program. She was a weak student and had failed out. Even so, her English had been much better back then. But everyone thought that she had long ago returned to China with her physicist husband and their young son.

Where was she calling from?

A hospital, it developed. A hospital in St. John's. She needed help. At least that's what Duffett thought she was asking for. The voice faded out and the line went dead.

Duffett made some phone calls of his own. Soon he was talking to a cheerful-sounding doctor with a British accent. "Ah, the university. At least we know that much now. Bit of a mystery woman, you see. Couldn't figure out what she was doing here."

What was wrong with her? Duffett asked.

"Wrong? Well, she weighs about seventy pounds, for one thing. Habitual expression is a vacant stare. You've seen photographs of concentration camp survivors?"

She'd been brought to the hospital by paramedics summoned by police, who'd been called to an address on LeMarchant Road, a rooming house whose tenants were welfare recipients and foreign students. Someone had reported water flowing out of a common bathroom whose door was locked. The police had found the woman unconscious in the tub.

We have no idea, the doctor said, how or why she got into this state. Perhaps Duffett, since he acknowledged having some connection with her, wouldn't mind dropping by the LeMarchant address to see if there was information to be gleaned? After which he would come to the hospital himself, of course.

Duffett co-opted Wilson Quong, one of our contractuals, perhaps the world's unlikeliest Jane Austen scholar.

The rooming house was a labyrinth whose population was only marginally more articulate than the woman in the hospital. No one admitted knowing anything about her, including the caretaker, who was bribed into allowing Duffett and Quong into her room.

The furniture consisted of a cot, blood-stained and befouled, and a chest of drawers, on top of which lay some documents. These included thirty-four uncashed cheques for $168 each, a form indicating that rent was to be paid directly to the landlord by social services, and a letter identifying the woman's next of kin as someone named Todd Butt.

There were also three suitcases. One contained food – dry pasta, cooking oil, that sort of thing. A second held an array of cheap, oddly frivolous-seeming objects, trinkets made of plastic, mostly, the kind of article you'd find in a dollar store. Gifts, Duffett concluded. Presents that you give to someone whose help you may need, a government official, say, in order to establish good relations, a gesture of courtesy.

The third suitcase contained more documents, these written in Chinese. Quong began to read them. Soon, Duffett noted, tears were sliding down his smooth cheeks.

The thing about these people, Duffett interjects here, the Chinese who came over after Tiananmen Square, scientists nearly all of them, is this. Failure was not an option. The honour of the PRC was on the line. More than that, the honour of every family whose son or daughter came over was on the line. If you failed, your family didn't want to hear about it. Or you.

Quong pieced together two stories from the documents, which were mostly letters from the woman's family and drafts of letters she had sent them. One of the stories was fiction. She was doing well here. Her husband was successful, their son a brilliant student. She herself was still in the program (ten years later, Duffett commented) but expected to complete her degree very soon. She was very happy.

The other story was not fiction. After she had failed, and her husband had completed his own degree, he had deserted her, taking their child with him. There was a piece of paper with his name on it, and an address somewhere in New England. There were two or three harshly worded letters from him, none recent. There was a photo album, featuring a boy who might have been two or three. Some were dated, six or seven years ago.

I can't emphasize too strongly, Duffett says, how badly this place stank. The whole building stank, her room worst of all.

Duffett is not the sort of man to be ruled by emotion. So his account of the reunion at the hospital is minimalist. The woman was glad to see him. She looked even worse than the doctor had led him to believe. She was glad, too, to meet and converse with Quong.

Quong phoned her family. They were wealthy, he reported, of the merchant class. They will take her back, he said. There was some doubt? Duffett asked him. Well, said Quong, they think she will be useful for teaching English to small children. So they will take her back. It was clear, Duffett said, that Quong appreciated the family's position on that point.

And from then on, the woman began to recover. A happy ending, Duffett says. I can see he's made himself angry.

Who was Todd Butt?

A social worker. She never cashed the cheques because she didn't know how to deal with banks.

So what did she do to stay alive?

Nobody knows, Duffett says. Quong couldn't get much out of her. Nobody really has a clue.

I think for a moment about Raissa's film, about the young woman who can't make herself understood. But I don't think Duffett would be interested, so I don't say anything.

Home. I note the absence of kid-related clutter in the front porch. Have the Mini-Maids been here? No, it's not their day. And there's nobody here, apparently, not a creature stirring. I check out the kitchen.

The note is brief and cordial. There are two main points: first, Emily has decided to move on, but this decision has nothing to do with me, and second, she'll be in touch, but in the meantime I should not attempt to find out where she is.

It's signed, *Love, E.*

Chapter Seven

It's two weeks or so later, and the world has changed. Maureen has been here a week now, her presence the result of a none-too-protracted round of negotiations that began the very evening of Emily's o'erhasty departure. Yes, there are mixed feelings, on her side too, I'd lay odds, but for now, we seem to have decided, without discussion, all the alternatives are worse. There have been no arguments. No one has taken offence. All's more or less right with the world.

Except of course for Emily, from whom nothing has been heard. My first reaction, on discovering what I've come to think of as her escape, was to call the police. But even as I reached for the phone I recognized this move as quixotic. She is, after all, an adult. Hard to acknowledge but technically true. A mother with two children has decided to pursue the good life in some location other than St. John's. Hardly a novel move, one likely to inspire a mutedly amused response by the polite voice at the police number. Instead I called Raissa McCloskey, who counselled passivity while claiming not to have been consulted by Emily before the fact nor to have been contacted since.

"Maybe she found living with you a bit much."

"What do you mean by that?"

"Just that you might not be the easiest person to get along with."

"A preposterous notion."

Raissa laughed, not unkindly. "Well, she's been under a lot of pressure–"

"Look, if you hadn't given me that clipping, she'd be here now."

"Is it so certain that she knew you had it?"

This stopped me in my tracks for a moment. I'd been taking it for granted. "Well, if she left it on your table on purpose, she'd be pretty certain you wouldn't keep it to yourself, wouldn't she? I mean, it's sort of like putting an ad in *The Telegram*."

We have a long tradition of such banter, Raissa and I. She chose not to respond in kind. "But seriously?"

"Okay, she leaves the clipping on your table. She knows that your loyalties are divided between us. No. Strike that. She thought that you would, correctly, recognize that what she really wanted was to tell me but couldn't bring herself to do it."

"You really think that's what she thought?"

"Yes." Only then did I realize that was exactly what I thought. "But why did she leave before I could speak to her about it, if that's what she really wanted?"

"But she was there when you came back with the clipping."

"Yes, but the kids–"

"Maybe the point was that you were supposed to override all that, and when you didn't make a dramatic scene out of it, she thought you didn't want to know, didn't really want the truth. Like you wanted to keep her at arm's length."

"How could she think that?"

"Maybe she saw it as another rejection, like when you wouldn't let her live with you after your marriage broke up."

Of course Emily would have given Raissa a complete account of that incident. No surprise there. Roll with the punch. "But the thing is, her coming here, I thought it was a chance for me to make up for that. That's what I wanted."

"Funny old world. But really, Hugh, it may be that she doesn't believe you really love her. Or at least isn't sure."

That was two weeks ago. Since then I've regarded Raissa – perhaps naively – as an ally in my quest for Emily. But though we've had several friendly exchanges since, she says she's as much in the dark as I am.

Foley, true to form, knows nothing either. I waited two days to call Sandra, not wishing to alarm her unduly, hoping that Emily would return immediately. But when I did call, she seemed more relieved than anything. "Well, she's probably better off elsewhere, isn't she? She may be coming here, where the environment for the children is more …" She hesitated, looking for the word that best combines diplomacy with insult, "… more *propitious* for them."

"But why isn't she there yet? If she's going to Ottawa, she must be flying. No way she could rent a car here at this time of year. And how could she book a flight so quickly?"

"Maybe she's visiting friends in Newfoundland. I agree it's worrying. But most likely she's still in St. John's, don't you think?"

But despite her promise to call when Emily got in touch, there has been no communication. And Sandra always keeps her word.

Of course there are other options – tracking down every last one of her local friends and grilling them, for example. But to what end? If Emily doesn't wish to be discovered, why not grant her that wish?

The signature event of our, Maureen's and my, life together so far is what could be called plumbing-related, even plumbocentric. Whether this is propitious or not I have yet to discern. Several days ago a notice appeared in the mailbox, informing us that the city was going to be doing something to the water mains along the street, and that it would be required that the water be shut off the next day from eight in the morning until five in the afternoon. Later the same day a city worker, hard-hatted and sweatily red-faced, rang the bell to make sure the notice had been received.

For most homeowners, I've been led to believe, shutting off the water is not a big deal. There should be one easily identifiable thing-you-turn on an easily identifiable pipe near the point at which said pipe enters the basement. You turn the appropriate thing and the water stops. Even as the worker was explaining that it was imperative that this be done *before* eight the next morning, I was recalling that, because of the odd layout of the house, the result of its having been half its present size a hundred years ago, then expanded in the forties, there might be some difficulty ahead – a difficulty compounded by my own ineptitude in simple practical matters.

Only the back half of the house sits on – or straddles? – a real basement. The front half has only a crawl space about two feet high. The basement proper has many pipes, many valves, many things that can be turned. It's been such a long time since the water has had to be turned off that I've forgotten which is the right one. The pipe enters from the front of the house, concealed in the eerie darkness of the crawl space. Who then knows what thingy to turn? I explained this, briefly, to the worker and asked if he'd mind having a look. He seemed pleased to be asked, perhaps wanting to cool off.

In the basement he scrutinized the array of pipes, valves, and things-that-you-turn. "It's none a these," he announced, voice authoritative and smug. "Must be through there." He pointed at the hole, a raggedy-edged cave entrance in the rocky wall, about five feet off the floor, through which one would have to wriggle to enter the crawl space. "Up to the front a the house. That's where you'll find 'er."

No I won't, I thought.

He peered through the hole in a cursory sort of way. "Can't see 'er from 'ere. You'll know 'er when you see 'er, though. You'll need a flashlight." He seemed inappropriately happy about delivering this insight. I could think of nothing to ask him.

The notice in the mailbox had implied that a range of horrible things could happen if the water was not turned off in a timely manner, things that would involve varieties of liquid vileness spewing into one's sinks, bathtubs, and showers.

Maureen was sympathetic when I explained what would have to be done. She insisted on checking out the hole herself, made commiserating noises when I commented – perhaps a bit fulsomely – on the dirty and awkward nature of the task that lay ahead. It occurred to me that this might be a way of scoring points with Maureen, this minor demonstration of competence in performing painful but essential household duties. Yes, disillusionment would come soon enough if we stayed together, but why not start things off on the right foot?

"Theseus and the minotaur," she said, getting into the spirit, I thought. "I'll give you a ball of string."

"More like Hercules and the Augean stables," I riposted, snappy as ever. "I'll come out covered in crap."

The subject receded into insignificance until about 2 a.m., when I wrenched myself out of a faux-sleep, making noises of distress loud enough to wake Maureen. I'd been, not dreaming exactly, but vividly fantasizing about crawling in the darkness under the house, unable to move back or turn around or raise my head more than an inch without bashing it, knowing the absurdity of the fantasy but powerless to resist its pull. Breathing in the dust. Stuck, inert, suffering, impotent. What the hell was the matter with me?

Which was pretty much what Maureen was asking, in polite, sleep-slurred tones. I recognized, I thought, a potential turning point. I could bullshit about an instantly forgotten nightmare, or I could tell the demeaning truth.

I chose the latter, though my motive remains unclear – to establish that honesty *über alles* will be our marching tune or to give Maureen an opportunity to perceive me as less of a man than she'd bargained for, someone who could be moved on from with nary a backward glance. Was that what I wanted in the depths of my labyrinthine heart?

Maureen, now wide awake, said, "I'll do it. You go back to sleep now."

"No, no, I'll do it."

"Don't be silly, I don't mind doing it."

"It's not fair to ask you to do it."

"*I'm* asking *you*."

And so forth, for five minutes or so, nothing officially decided. But Maureen had the upper hand, if that's the right metaphor. Have I irrevocably de-sexed myself in her eyes? Has some precious element of power been passed from me to her for no reason, or is that way of analyzing what's going on between us anachronistic, flat-earthy?

Two things were now certain, though. I was going to get a few hours of sound sleep, and, come morning, she was going to be the one squirming into the hole.

When I woke up, it was morning, early, and Maureen was nowhere in sight.

Perhaps she'd gone.

The first thought, oddly, was how quickly I could resign myself to that, followed by, that was selfish of her but maybe a clean break is best for both of us, followed by sadness at the thought that sex would no longer be readily available, followed by a flash of guilt inspired by the crassness of the previous thought softened by the self-righteous gut sense that there was nothing really wrong with that previous thought. Followed by a self-congratulatory feeling that my wellspring of delusional optimism would continue to produce such gems of rationalization no matter what, more evidence that despair will never cross my threshold, kept forever at bay by my trusty security guard, stupidity.

Then I heard a noise in the kitchen. Thank God, I haven't been abandoned after all. The figure at the kitchen table, sitting with its back to me, bending to adjust a rubber boot, was not at first recognizable. But it was Maureen, all right, dressed as for janneying. A floor-length heavy cotton dress, darkish blue relieved by small flowers of various colours, over it a stained blue sweatshirt, on the table my old Red Sox cap, beside a pink kerchief to be used, she was soon to explain, to protect her mouth against subterranean dust.

"I've been poking around in one of your closets."

As we proceeded through the ritual expostulations and disclaimers, I began to realize the magnanimity of the gesture. If I had un-manned myself conceptually with my nocturnal admission (ha ha) of wimphood, here she was de-sexing herself in a tangible, visually powerful way, as if to say: Here I am, a version of myself that mocks the conventional imagery that you're supposed to cherish – but the version that you happen to need this morning. Acknowledgement of necessity trumps illusion, as far as we're concerned. Doesn't it?

I quickly decided that witticisms, however innocuous, would be out of place. In short order we were proceeding, wordlessly, to the basement.

The hole presented itself like some parody of existential abyss-hood. Maureen clambered eagerly into it, or at least without hesitation, having used a small

stepladder to gain the requisite altitude. I passed her the
flashlight, she reaching back as though receiving a baton
in a relay race. There was nothing for me to do other
than hang out near the orifice like some weak imitator
of the guy in charge of Mission Control, terrified
that Maureen would soon be saying the equivalent of
"Houston, we've got a problem." Would I then be
honour-bound to plunge in after her? And then what if
I got stuck? No one else in the world would know we
were down here. No, I'd have to go for help, in the first
instance probably to the city work crew that, we'd
noticed, had already been positioning themselves in the
street, ready to begin their day precisely at eight.

And how embarrassing would that be, and how repre-
hensible was it that I was thinking of my embarrassment
when, after all, Maureen would – in this fantasy – be stuck
underneath the house alone, while I was gone, and
how the workers would be saying things like "Couldn't
get under there yourself, buddy?" and the like.

In the meantime a voice in my head was saying,
"We have liftoff," an observation I thought it best to keep
to myself.

"Can you see it?" I asked, fearing loss of contact.

"No."

"Are you sure?"

"Yes."

"The guy yesterday said he thought it might be over
to the right."

Was this in fact true? I wasn't sure, but found the
possibility at least credible.

"Over to the right? Just a minute … No. No, there's
nothing."

"Nothing at all?"

There followed a silence of the sort often recorded in fiction as an em dash in quotation marks.

Then Maureen said, "I'm coming out" at the precise moment at which I said, "Come out." And there she was, crawling backward, one of the things that, in my dream, I feared I wouldn't be able to do. She did it in a way that seemed to say, "Nothing to it," a regular well-co-ordinated series of movements that led to the reappearance of, first, the rubber boots, then the blue of the cotton dress, now somewhat scarred by streaks of dirt, then the rest of her emerging inexorably in (it struck me) a wacky send-up of a breech birth, the head revealing itself last as I stood by pretending to be ready to offer assistance, inexperienced spotter for Maureen as she completed some hitherto unknown gymnastic event.

Maureen pulled the kerchief away from her face. She then said, "Fuck."

The rest is anti-climactic, though perhaps from her perspective requiring greater courage than she had already demonstrated. She marched outside, approached the nearest cluster of workmen, unconcerned, clearly, about the impression her spelunking garb might create. I hovered discreetly in the doorway as she spoke animatedly to the foreman.

He followed her back inside, down to the basement, nodding as he passed me in the hallway, as if to say, "Couldn't get under there yourself, buddy?"

I didn't bother following them, but after about ten seconds I heard him say, "It's this one here."

It turned out that the man who had come around the day before was a new hire, someone who, remarkably, was as ignorant as I am about what makes things function.

Ray McGuire has been in touch. He's made good on his promise to contact the ex-Oblate who knew Cleary, one Charlie Moran, now a philosophy prof, as well as baseball fan and golfer, apparently the original point of contact between him and Ray. "He was really interested to know somebody was working on Cleary's novels," Ray told me the next day. "He's never read them, just heard about them. I guess they weren't a hot topic in Oblate-land. But he said he knew him pretty well in the period before he went missing." And then, a couple of sentences later, the payoff: Moran had agreed to do a taped interview with him. Which arrived a couple of days ago.

Moran's voice on the tape has an odd quality, a kind of confidential but earnest colloquial tone, the sentences punctuated by interjections such as "geez" and "ya know," mixed with the vocabulary appropriate to the holder of a doctorate from Fordham. In the first part of the interview, Ray establishes that Moran knew Cleary for about five years before the presumed murder, and that Cleary had been influential in causing him to question his own vocation and ultimately to renounce it. At one point Ray asks Moran about their relationship.

McGuire: So you and Father Cleary were friends?

Moran: Geez, that's hard to say, ya know. I don't know if the concept of friendship was really relevant to Phonse's way of dealing with the world. We did spend a lot time in dialogue, I'll say that.

McGuire: So what was he like to talk with?

Moran: I'd say abrasive, ya know, but abrasive and liberating at the same time. And funny. He'd say anything to get a rise out of people. I remember one time there was a symposium on Thomas Merton, and he got up and said, "Theologically, Merton was a bit of a cockteaser, wasn't he?" You can imagine how that went over. Didn't bother him, though. He picked his spots. And he knew no one around here could lay a glove on him. Another time somebody gave a lecture on the Blessed Virgin. In the question period, Phonse says, "When is the bachelors' club in the Vatican going to address the feminine beyond Mary in plaster-of-Paris?" Caused a bit of a stir.

McGuire: So he wasn't popular with his superiors?

Moran: That's putting it mildly, Ray. They would've loved to get rid of him. Ya know, nobody could figure out why he didn't quit. He'd just say, "I've been priesting it for twenty years" – or whatever – "so why stop now?"

McGuire: So this story about his murder …

Moran: Well, we don't know it was murder, right, Ray, because no body was ever found. Let's say it was convenient for people to *regard* it as murder. Or death by misadventure. Or any kind of death, right?

McGuire: What happened?

Moran: Geez, Ray, nobody knows, do they? The order bought him this new van, see, so he could go to California on his sabbatical.

McGuire: The order bought him a van?

Moran: Ya, brand new, he insisted on it. See, he never put up a fuss about turning his salary over to them.

Not like some.

McGuire: What do you mean?

Moran: Well, when we joined up with that godless secular institution, a lot of the guys were making real money for the first time in their lives. Automatically members of the faculty union, see? They wanted to cash those paycheques themselves, if you know what I mean. There was some unpleasantness, even, let's say, some defections. But not Phonse.

McGuire: Okay, so they bought him this van.

Moran: Ya, they did. Ya know, Ray, they were thinking, He's off to California, we won't have to deal with him for a year. Good riddance. Then old Warpy Casey gets this call from the police in Colorado, I think it was. The van was found abandoned. No sign of Phonse.

McGuire: Warpy?

Moran: Yeah, geez, I'd almost forgotten. That was the nickname Phonse hung on him. Not to his face, right? But Warpy was what you'd call old school, and Phonse had a sort of jaundiced view of the way he did things. Yeah, jaundiced. Of course he would've had problems with any superior.

McGuire: So they found the van.

Moran: Ya, and like I say there was no indication of what happened, right, they just found this van in the parking lot of a motel somewhere. When the cops called Warpy, he said, Well, do what you can, fellas, sort of thing and then kind of lost interest, officially. So I don't think they ever pursued it. I mean, nobody was too anxious to find Phonse Cleary by this point in his priestly career, if you catch my drift.

McGuire: That's kind of cold and uncaring, isn't it?

Moran: Ya, so what's your point, Ray? [laughs, a dry, brittle chuckle]

McGuire: So there was no trace of him, no clues, no leads?

Moran: Nothing. Except there was a note on the front seat of the van, just a phrase, meant nothing to anyone.

McGuire: Do you remember what it was?

Moran: Geez, Ray, it's been a long time. It was something like "If not perdiculum then kill Rassleman." That's not it, but something like it.

[Listening for the first time, I stopped the tape here and played back that speech to make sure I'd heard correctly, because "Perdicaris alive or Raisuli dead" is a phrase that plays a crucial role in Cleary's third novel, *Saucers over the Vatican*, in circumstances remarkably parallel to his own real-life disappearance. Neither McGuire nor Moran was, of course, in a position to make the connection.]

McGuire: So there was no trace after that? Nobody used his credit cards or his ID or anything?

Moran: Nothing. That was it for Father Phonse Cleary. For PR purposes, the order's position was that there must've been foul play. I mean, why would anyone choose to disappear that way, right? So that was picked up by the press here, and nobody ever questioned it.

McGuire: And nobody cared enough to follow up?

Moran: Not enough to go out to Colorado.

McGuire: So what happened to the stuff he left behind, his papers and that?

Moran: Ya, well, that's the thing, Ray, there wasn't much. He must've taken it all with him. Or destroyed it all. He'd cleared out his office at the university, too, because of the sabbatical. It was almost like he'd never been here.

The tape ends shortly after this point. I've been replaying it obsessively. Quite apart from the content, there's something disconcerting about listening to someone who actually knew Cleary, like watching a figure in a museum burst out of its glass case. How carefully I've kept my knowledge of Cleary's novels and the few facts of his biography apart from my own daily life. Why have I never tried to contact the Oblates, to find out what he left behind or whether anyone would agree to talk about him? Is it that I've wanted to be alone with the sacred texts, like playing some elaborate board game, enjoying my own private Clearydom?

This time Raissa is waiting for me at the coffee place, or emporium, or whatever the correct term is. "Shop" is clearly too humble and utilitarian. I notice her immediately; partly it's the hair, but also the fact that she's pointing a video camera in my direction.

Resisting the impulse to shield my face with a forearm, I approach warily. She's called to say she has news of Emily but wants to deliver it in person.

"What's up? Why are you doing that?"

She lays the camera on the table.

"I think," she says, "I can get funding to do a sort of reality-based half-hour docudrama. And you could be in it. Or maybe someone playing you. But I just want to get enough material to give them the idea."

"Why would I be in it?"

"Okay, here's the premise. It would be about people

who get unexpected news about other people who are important to them, given by an off-camera third person, such as me."

"And?"

"So I'm about to tell you something about Emily. You don't mind, do you?" She repositions the camera threateningly as she speaks. Then she presses a button.

"So," I say with deliberate woodenness, "I have come to find out what you have to tell me about Emily."

"I can cut that later. Okay. Emily phoned me last night."

I wait.

"Can we try that again? Try to ditch the deer in the headlights look. It's cliché. Do something interesting with your eyes."

"For Christ's sake, will you just tell me what Emily said? Is she all right?"

"That's better. I like the passion there. Once more. 'Emily phoned me last night.'"

It can't be that bad, or she wouldn't be doing this. Would she?

"O my god. After all these years. I thought she died in the avalanche in Peru."

"Okay, you're a lost cause. Yes, of course she's all right. Do you think I'd put you through this if she wasn't?"

"Probably."

She considers this. "Weren't you the one who told us to ruthlessly exploit others in the service of art?"

She has me there. Who would have thought that she – or anyone – would take me seriously?

"Where was she calling from?"

"I don't know. She wouldn't say. She's all right. The kids are all right. She asked me to tell you that."

"That's *it*?"

She nods. She must know more than she's saying. But she doesn't flinch at my stare. Instead she insists on getting the coffee.

"Do me a favour. Shoot me coming back to the table, and then say, 'Aaron Spracklin dropped dead yesterday.'"

I do as I'm told.

She doesn't acknowledge my line, instead focuses on carefully placing the cups on the table. Then looks directly at the camera and says, as with mild amusement, "So what's your point?" Then she motions for me to turn the camera off. "Aaron will enjoy that."

"Isn't he the guy who was stalking you?"

"Well, it's not *stalking* stalking, it's more like playing at stalking, if you know what I mean. He knows I'm *happily married.*" She waggles her wedding-beringed finger at me. "Still, I think he does have a bit of a thing for me. Understandably." She grins, savouring both the irony and the truth underlying it. "And he *was* good in *Speaking in Tongues*, so I wouldn't mind working with him again. He's really talented, actually. He's in a band, too. The Zulu Tolstoys. Maybe you've heard of them?"

"A tad underneath my radar, I fear. By the way, does he have a nickname?"

She looks puzzled. I explain about my David-not-Dave theory.

"No. I guess with a name like Aaron, you really can't. I mean, can you imagine someone saying, 'Oh yeah, Aaron Spracklin, I know him so well I call him

Aa'? I don't think so."

"In any case, can we get back to Emily? There must be *some*thing more she said that could give us some clue–"

"But there wasn't. There really wasn't. It's some bizarre, hey? Your daughter on the lam. And we don't know why, if she's actually broken the law or what. Don't you think there's something, well, Pynchonesque about it?"

"I think of it more in terms of gritty realism."

"Yeah, but the sunglasses, the two women involved, the witnesses. It doesn't seem real to me. And who was the guy? What was that all about? You know, when we have all the facts, I bet it'll make a great story."

CHAPTER EIGHT

Unlike Emily, Terry Foley has decided to stick around. "Returning to Vancouver," he said in one of several calls, "given my current financial status ... well, I fear it's out of the question for the time being."

That last phrase is typical Foley, too, the implication being that in the fullness of time his "current financial status" will be miraculously upgraded without his having to lift the proverbial finger.

There was then a short pause designed to allow us to meditate on his poverty, and, more specifically, to allow me the opportunity to offer him a loan. When I stay silent, he starts up again. "I can continue to work on the thesis here. The basic research is done. The library is more or less adequate for my purposes. As for my accommodation issues, there's good news. I've found suitable digs."

I can't let that one pass. "Figs? Suitable for what?"

Foley apparently concludes that there's a problem with my hearing. "Digs," he shouts. "Living quarters. As you might have guessed, the arrangement is not unconnected to the young woman you saw me with on Signal Hill some time back. Not, of course, that there can be anything between us."

"Of course."

"Perhaps we could get together soon for a small libation."

"Perhaps."

"I have some ideas I'd like to run by you. My impecuniousness is causing many practical difficulties."

"As long as you understand that your impecuniousness will not diminish at the expense of my bank account."

"Duly noted."

I stand in Barney Power's office doorway. If I go in, I may not be able to get away for half an hour.

"You heard about your man, did you?"

This is a standard opening conversational gambit for Barney. There's no way of knowing who one's "man" is nor what he is supposed to have done. One's only possible response, short of rudely shutting things down, is to ask who.

"Who?"

A rolling of the eyes. The answer is always supposed to have been obvious. "Stiggins."

"What's he done now?"

"Close the door."

I comply.

He waves at a chair. "Rest your holy and blessed. Move that box out of the way, will you?"

The banker's box is inscribed "Lebanese material" in black marker.

"I have three articles in progress this summer," he says, with an absolutely straight face, as though daring me to contradict him. "Coming right out of that box."

Barney's "Lebanese material" has, over the last five or six years, become a staple of departmental banter. At a certain point the administration managed to negotiate a clause in the collective agreement to the effect that faculty who don't engage in research are required to teach an extra course. Desperate to avoid this fate, the notoriously unproductive Barney had within weeks let it be known that he had embarked on an ambitious new project: a cultural history of the Lebanese community in Newfoundland. The facts that such a study has nothing to do with our discipline and that Barney is completely unqualified to carry it out have been politely overlooked, officially – however much unofficial merriment they have inspired.

And Barney has indeed done much grunt-work, interviewing every person in Newfoundland known to have a drop of Lebanese blood. ("My head feels Basha-ed in" has become his favourite witticism, referring to one of the most common Newfoundland Lebanese surnames.) He has applied for and received the services of a series of graduate student assistants, who have catalogued every byte of information under several different headings each. On one occasion he's been able to get *out* of teaching a course because of his unusually heavy research load. All this without having published a syllable.

And the strange thing is, everyone knows it's a scam. But it's not in anyone's interest to cause trouble. *It's Barney. He's harmless. Let him pretend.* The pretence bothers me only at this personal level, at which it becomes necessary, as now, to appear to take Barney seriously when he says he's going to have three articles written by the end of the summer – even though he knows that I know that he knows ….

"Good for you," I say. True to form, Barney doesn't ask about my own research activities. While other colleagues might inquire out of politeness, Barney sees no need to pretend.

"Stiggins has named me," he says. "I'm considering legal action."

"Named you?"

"Look at this." He thrusts a piece of paper into my hand. It's a memo sent by Stiggins to Alice Plover, in her role as chair of the Search Committee. "I've marked the offensive passage."

The memo, I note, is dated sometime in February. Its purpose was to comment on one of the applicants for our new postcolonial position, Delia Lovenguth. As is customary for shortlisted candidates, she gave a public lecture. Members of the department were invited to evaluate her performance. Stiggins has written, in the passage marked by Barney, that "Dr. Lovenguth handled herself with aplomb in response to the vigorous interrogation by Dr. Power, responding calmly and convincingly to his rudely interjected questions."

For some reason, Barney has a bee in his bonnet about the very notion of postcoloniality. I remember the department meeting some fifteen years ago when the decision was made to change the titles of a couple of courses from "Commonwealth" to "Postcolonial." Barney was the lone dissenter, his hand held stoically aloft as the new terminology was approved by something like forty-three to one. Of course part of Barney's opposition had to do with the fact that the change was being proposed by Mark Silverstein, demon publisher and student favourite, who has long since departed for greener pastures on the mainland. But there was probably more to it than that. With Barney, there always is.

In any case, Barney's disdain for Delia Lovenguth's subject erupted during her presentation. Discussing J. M. Coetzee's *Foe*, she was taking the improbable position that it's not possible to discern from the text whether Friday has a tongue or not. Maybe he does have a tongue and has decided not to use it. This seemed to enrage Barney, who, uncharacteristically, interrupted several times to heckle Delia, suggesting – wittily as he no doubt thought – that perhaps her point was that the cat had got Friday's tongue. There was an embarrassed silence. Delia smiled back at him, serenely carrying on with the ingenious analysis that in the end won her the job. Rupert Stiggins was not alone in thinking that Barney had made a fool of himself, though probably no one else would say so to the committee.

"Barney, this happened about six months ago. Why the fuss now?"

"It was given to me only yesterday," Barney says, grimly.

It dawns on me that Stiggins is known to be a supporter of Reg Pike, and that Alice Plover must have given the document to Barney.

"Barney, I don't see what the basis for legal action would be here."

"You think it's all right for him to ridicule me publicly and get away with it."

"Well, he's not *ridiculing* you, he's just describing what he thinks happened. And it's not supposed to be a *public* document anyway."

"You think I was rude at the lecture?"

"I think you were somewhat aggressive, given the context. I mean, a candidate is pretty much defenceless in that situation."

Barney snorts. I don't deserve an answer. "You see, if he'd said, 'the vigorous interrogation by *one colleague*,' I wouldn't object. But he identified me by name."

"But Barney, everyone on the committee would have known it was you anyway."

"That's neither here nor there." Discerning that I'm not going to support him in his madness, Barney has lost interest in pursuing the subject. He'll corner someone potentially more sympathetic later on. (Good luck with that one.) "I'll tell you one thing. If Reg Pike gets in, Rupert Stiggins will have a major influence in running this department."

A most unlikely scenario, as Stiggins has no interest in anything but his own career, defined in terms of publications, conference papers – the more exotic the locale, the better – and grants. Probably he's made the rational calculation that a Pike headship will simply be less annoying than a Plover-led regime. Many, including me, would agree with him about this, if nothing else.

"Stiggins," Barney says reflectively.

I sense an anecdote coming on. "Barney, I'm going to have to leave now."

"We've had visitors from out of town. Last Saturday we're driving along Military Road. In front of the Basilica, my friend says, 'Look at the old tramp,' so I look, and you know what I said?"

"No, Barney, I don't." But I do, I do.

"I said to him, 'That's my colleague Rupert Stiggins.' And it was. He was wearing–"

"Barney, I'm outta here. Nature calls."

I've heard several different versions of this story over the years, the identity of the tramp-like colleague varying from telling to telling. And I have a credible second-hand report to the effect that, on at least one occasion, the tramp was me.

An hour later, about half the department has convened in a classroom, our first meeting in preparation for the review, which is to begin in earnest in September, after Greg Harkness's reign has ended, and Alice or Reg has taken over. Harkness looks even more genial than he usually does on such occasions. Presiding over this meeting will be one of his last public acts as head. He beams at us all indiscriminately.

He tells us that, as a first step in the review process, the vice-president has asked that we address the question of how the department's "collective sense of its present and future self" squares with the university's mission statement, copies of which have been distributed before the meeting. The predictable hubbub of groans, chortles, and various other noises connoting disaffection ensues. Harkness's grin becomes broader as the room quiets down. "Any ideas as to how we should do this?"

Barney yawns loudly, causing a few titters. It's impossible to know whether he's done it on purpose.

Alice Plover, not unexpectedly, has some ideas, though, as usual, they're hard for her audience to grasp. She has a droning, repetitive speaking style that causes people to tune out shortly after she begins to hold forth. The result is that she often gets her way; others won't challenge her in order to avoid having to pretend to listen to her answers.

"… very unique geographic, cultural, and economic milieu …" she is saying, then, "set in order the prioritization of our pedagogic goals … maintenance of our traditional … " And, as usual, at a certain point she seems to fear interruption and begins to speak more quickly, her voice rising as though to overcome her silent opponents before they can get a word out. Then she stops, and it's pin-drop time. What has she said?

Whatever it was, there were a lot of solecisms.

After a moment, Victoria Bickerstaff pipes up. "I absolutely agree with every point Alice has just made …."

Home to Maureen, the woman who has defined herself as She Who Has Crawled under the House for Me. A good start, but what's next? She greets me with a smile and a hug of the sort that suggests, "This is a hug and that's all it is. It will not, for the moment, lead to anything further." Something about the nature of the squeeze – authoritative though affectionate – and the precision with which it's terminated, no lingering connection. Fair enough, though somehow sad. The damn-the-torpedoes passion of the illicit will never again be ours. No delicious frenzy of the uncertain: How much time do we have? Will he/she/they find out? When, if ever, will this happen again? No, it's all placidity and let's-wait-till-later, an attitude more becoming to middle-aging co-habitors.

"So," she says. "Honey, you're home." And then, after the perfunctory snickers, "I know."

Saucers over the Vatican, Cleary's third novel, is a satirical attack on the secrecy, intellectual bankruptcy, and hypocrisy of the contemporary Roman Catholic Church. It should have got him defrocked, or whatever the appropriate technical term is. In fact, it most probably never came to the attention of those in the hierarchy. Or perhaps it did, and they calculated that to make a fuss, given the obscurity of the author and his press, would be counterproductive. So Tom Wetmore surmised in his own recently published but already-remaindered memoir *Apostle to the Philistines: How Canada Failed Me*, described in the *Globe* review as "vintage venom from the embittered old gadfly."

The protagonist is a young priest doing research in a Vatican library. Cleary does little to make the setting, characters, and plot believable; it's all parable all the way. By page five, Father Peter O'Neill has stumbled upon a misplaced "forbidden" file that refers obliquely to the appearance of the Virgin Mary at Fatima as "a staged event making use of our standard sacred technology." O'Neill's innocence and sincerity – mocked by Cleary's prose in virtually every sentence – inspire him to collect enough evidence to convince the world of Fatima's fakery, and thereby purge the Church of the unspiritual elements that – naively, naively, Cleary would have the reader believe – must be separated from its authentically Christian core.

Cleary's premise, that there's a suspicious symmetry between the reported details of the Fatima miracle and accounts of encounters of ordinary people with UFOs, was not original with him. In fact, in a brief endnote he acknowledges his indebtedness to the renowned and – atypically – sane UFO researcher Jacques Vallee, who, in a book published several years before *Saucers over the Vatican*, had pointed out a number of such similarities. These included such phenomena present at Fatima as the trance-state of the percipients, the appearance of a transparent white cloud, a white light gliding above the treetops, the presence of a powerful, mysterious wind, a bright flash, a buzzing or humming sound, the sun morphing into a flat disk exuding beams of coloured light, a strange fragrance, a heat wave as the disk descended in its zig-zag, "falling leaf" motion, and so on. Many of these elements, Vallee argued, are common denominators of standard accounts of UFO sightings.

Cleary's twist on this idea was not only that such "miracles" as Fatima are engineered by the Church, but also that what the secret file refers to as "the forces of the Adversary" make use of the same secret knowledge. For O'Neill, the only moral course of action is to reveal the truth, the whole truth, to the world. But how to do so credibly?

He decides to find the place where the technology is housed, assemble incontrovertible proof of its existence, and disseminate the knowledge through the media. Fortunately he has an ally, a journalist with whom, through a chance meeting, he has made friends, and who, it turns out, has long suspected that the Church has harboured such a secret. They work together, using hints from documents in the forbidden file, to narrow the search. Soon their activities attract attention. A sinister monsignor is suspicious of O'Neill; his journalist friend believes he is being watched. O'Neill travels to a number of different cities in Europe, ostensibly to further his legitimate research but in fact to collect further information on "the Fatima conspiracy."

Cleary keeps the action moving quickly, never missing an opportunity for an incidental satirical thrust at the Church. O'Neill begins to receive death threats, though it's not clear whether the source is the sinister monsignor or the forces of the Adversary, or both. He comes to believe that he may have to fake his death and assume a new identity. But he arranges to give his friend a signal that he is alive and that it's now time to publish their revelations before the journalist, too, becomes a target. The signal is to be a postcard bearing a cryptic phrase. And here is the point at which fiction intersects with Cleary's life: the cryptic phrase is "Perdicaris alive or Raisuli dead."

So Cleary deliberately walked away from his life as a priest and left a message decipherable only by those who (a) know his work intimately, and (b) care enough about his life to stumble across the information about the note in the van. Whom did he think would fit both categories? Has he somehow imagined me into existence? Is he still alive? Does he want me to find him?

Saucers over the Vatican comes to a climax when Father O'Neill discovers the location, though not the secret, of the hardware that constitutes the "sacred technology" – a huge underground installation somewhere in the Alps. Shortly after he passes the information on to his journalist friend, he is hunted down by a hit man. With typical Cleary-esque irony, his life is saved when the assassin's bullet lodges in the New Testament he always carries close to his heart. Is such a thing remotely credible? In this sort of fiction, it doesn't matter.

O'Neill fakes his death successfully – car plunging over a cliff, bursting into flames, standard Hollywood sacred technology. In the last sentence of the main part of the narrative, he drops a postcard into a mailbox, turns away, and walks toward a railway station. There is a brief epilogue. The journalist uses the information that he and O'Neill have gathered to write a novel titled *The Fatima Conspiracy*. It becomes an international bestseller despite – or because of – the Vatican's vigorous repudiation of its content. But no one believes it can be true. The journalist is last seen in an upscale restaurant in Rome, sharing a meal with an unidentified man who is almost certainly the sinister monsignor. In the novel's last paragraph, O'Neill, who seems now to be living in St. John's, is browsing in a bookstore. He picks up a copy of *The Fatima Conspiracy* and flips through it, smiling grimly.

"Perdicaris alive or Raisuli dead." I recall checking that out when I first read *Saucers over the Vatican*. The words of a telegram sent by John Hay, Teddy Roosevelt's Secretary of State, from the Republican Party convention of 1904. A former resident of New Jersey named Ion

Perdicaris, who was then living in Morocco, was kidnapped by a local warlord named Raisuli, who demanded a $70,000 ransom. The telegram was meant to broadcast the fact that the US took seriously any overseas threats to its citizens' well-being, that American sovereignty could be exercised effectively in any remote, exotic locale. An assertion of Yankee power at the beginning of the new century. Evidently it got a lot of press at the time.

But things weren't quite what they at first seemed to be. Perdicaris turned out not to be an American citizen. He also got along well with Raisuli, in whose revolutionary cause he came to believe. The ransom was paid. Perdicaris remained alive, and Raisuli didn't have to die. American honour was officially upheld.

What any of this had to do with *Saucers over the Vatican* or Cleary's real life disappearance has remained unclear to me. In the novel, O'Neill's only stated reason for choosing it is that he likes the sound. The best comment I could muster for my monograph is that O'Neill, in faking his death, is identifying with the dark Other, the amoral, unknown, anarchic Raisuli side of his personality. And of course, repudiating his priestly vocation, to live an unexplored afterlife on a remote island.

Which raises the question of the extent to which that template fits Cleary's own biography.

"What's it like?" Maureen asks. "To read, I mean. Is it any good? I mean, I guess it must be or you wouldn't be into it, but ..." She's too polite to end the sentence.

It's not a question I'm ready to answer. Cleary's my obsession, *sui generis*. But after I've thought about it, I say, "It's sort of Richlerian."

"Richlerian? You mean the *Duddy Kravitz* guy?"

"No, I mean more like the *Solomon Gursky Was Here* guy. Or the *Barney's Version* guy. The guy who loved to stick it in and give it a twist. Not many Canadian writers do that. Think of Cleary as a Newfoundland Catholic version of Richler."

"But nobody reads him."

"They haven't had a chance. I'm doing my best."

"Right, you're going to publish something about him that nobody will read. And you've got this theory that he's still alive, which may be the only thing about him that people will be interested in. So why not write about his life? How come you've never tried to connect with anyone here who might know something about him?"

"Probably because it's easier to deal with books than people."

It's later, almost bedtime, when the phone rings.

"Hello?"

"Dad."

"Emily? Where are you are you okay are the kids all right?"

"Everything's fine, Dad. There's no need to worry."

I note the typically Emily generalization – "There's no need" – as opposed to the more obvious and normal "Don't worry." Ongoing conditions are such that no worry is required. She gets this from Sandra, of course, along with so much else.

"Okay, I'm not worrying. But give me some information, please. Where are you, for starters?"

"It doesn't matter where. We're safe, truly. But I need to ask you something."

"What?"

"Those phone calls I'd get from the woman I wouldn't tell you about?"

"Yes?"

"Have you been getting them since I left?"

I have to think about this. I suppose not. Like Ryan and Samantha, like the Serbian babysitters, like soccer and Ms. Frizzle, like the entire apparatus of Emily's month-long occupation, they've simply disappeared. "No, I haven't." And I regret saying it immediately. That piece of news was the only bargaining chip I had. "Don't hang up."

"Why would I hang up?"

Because, I think but don't say, it would be right in character. Instead I do say, "Raissa gave me the thing from the newspaper. About the hit-and-run in Vancouver. As you knew she would."

A silence. Then, "Yes." Spoken resentfully, as in an admission of guilt.

Two questions attempt to emerge from my mouth simultaneously. "Why didn't you tell me?" and "Which of the two women are you?" Of course I know the answer to the first – "I never tell you anything; why should this be different?" – and fear the answer to the second. In the end, I say simply, "Why?"

"I needed to tell you, but I couldn't."

"Why couldn't you?"

"Because" – and here her voice breaks, unusual but

not unprecedented for her (and she's probably been drinking) – "because you're always so negative about everything I've ever done. You'd push me away. Again. So I did it for you."

This is followed by a sort of blubbery sound. The phrase "burst into tears" isn't really appropriate, with its implication of a single watery explosion. It's more a matter of a series of not-quite-repressed seismic events followed by a certain amount of leakage. A major point of differentiation between mother and daughter: Sandra would neither blubber nor leak.

What she has said is of course patently untrue. Me, negative? About her? When? Yes, choosing Foley as a husband was a major gaffe – and not in my estimation alone – but apart from that? Yes, there was the time she was referring to, after the break-up with Sandra when I didn't want her around, but that was more than a decade ago, and had to do with my own fragile psychological state at the time; no negative judgment of her was stated or implied. Innocent, Your Honour. Or at least Not Guilty.

"Emily, I don't think that's entirely fair."

"I have to go now," she says, and before I can react, she's hung up. Several seconds go by before I think to put the receiver down.

Later I give Maureen a synopsis.

"What is it with you and women? You've got real talent for driving us away, don't you?"

"Thank you for that tall cool glass of astringency."

"True, isn't it? First, Sandra. Then Emily. Then me. Now Emily again. Who knows how many others?"

"That was then and this is now."

"Seriously, though, maybe it's good that she's saying it instead of just thinking it."

"Maybe."

She gives my hand a soft squeeze. The right one, the one that advertises my deformity. Once again Life demonstrating its ability to imitate Bad Art.

CHAPTER NINE

"I'm afraid," Foley is saying, "that something has developed between us after all."

He's speaking of the woman I saw him with on Signal Hill. Her name is Anna, he's told me, Anna Walmsley.

"So. Anna."

"Yes, well you know how it is. The friend of a friend. House in the Battery. Had a spare room. Agreed to put me up for a few days. The rest, I fear, is history."

"You fear."

"A figure of speech. I felt the need to qualify the statement somewhat, insert that phrase, as though to place myself in the role of relatively detached observer, responding to a situation over which I have no control."

Vintage Foley. He controls his words but not his actions. Is aware of it and satisfied with it? Is this what makes us kindred spirits?

"And you're telling me this why?"

Foley twists the end of his mustache before replying. "I wanted to make sure that everything is open and above board between us. You *are* Emily's father, after all–"

"Not the least of my accomplishments," I say, unable

to resist interrupting him, pompous git that he can be.

"And," he soldiers on, "I saw that look you gave us that time on Signal Hill. With your female companion. Not bad for her age, by the way."

"What look?"

He pauses, as if weighing the pros and cons of continuing. "I won't attempt to demonstrate. Your features became ... well, mildly contorted. It was a look that seemed to connote ... condemnation."

"I see." Though of course I don't, not really. "Odd coincidence. Just last night Emily was saying how negative I am."

"You spoke with Emily?"

"Yep."

"Where is she? How is she? How are the kids?"

"In order: I don't know; she's okay; they're okay. It was a very brief conversation."

"Did she mention me at all?"

"No, Foley, your name did not bubble to the surface at any point during our thirty second dialogue. Apparently your name wasn't high enough on Emily's agenda." In other circumstances this would be cruel – as would the calculatedly offhand mention of Emily's call – but this is a son-in-law who has just been boasting about having launched an affair. He has the grace to flinch slightly as I deliver the blow.

"I see."

"I'm not sure that you do. And I'm sure I don't. I still have no idea what's really going on. Foley, before Emily left Vancouver, did she say anything about a traffic accident, or more like a deliberate hit-and-run?"

He looks puzzled. "No. You mean someone hit

her? I'd know about that, wouldn't I?" Then it registers: "She deliberately knocked someone down?" He can't believe it any more than I can.

"Not necessarily." And thinking I have little to lose, I tell Foley about the newspaper clipping and the circumstances of its coming into my possession.

When I've finished he says, pensively, "Raissa McCloskey. You know, I think she had a bit of a thing for me once. Never came to anything. Of course that's hardly the point, is it? In any case. No, that story doesn't ring any bells."

I then tell him about Emily's mysterious phone calls.

"Probably Velma," he says.

"Who's Velma?"

"I can't say much about who Velma is."

"Give it a shot."

"Well, she was a friend of Emily's. I never actually met her myself. Spoke to her on the phone a few times. The abrupt manner seems characteristic. Emily said she wasn't really like that in person."

"So Emily knew her from where?"

"The Children's Library."

"What?"

"They have a program for pre-schoolers at the local public library. Emily would help out. So did Velma."

"And so?"

"That's it. That's pretty much all I know. They'd meet for coffee. No idea what they talked about."

I lay out my theory – that this Velma must somehow have corrupted Emily, seduced or bullied her into either committing, or at least being accomplice to, a serious crime.

Foley peers into the depths of his now-empty pint mug, then looks up to deliver his verdict: "Seems implausible on the face of it. Emily wouldn't do that kind of thing, would she – even in the service of a valid political cause." The oddly prurient gleam in his eye makes it clear that he can think of all sorts of valid political causes that might impel *him* to take such action.

"What about some non-political cause?"

"What do you mean?" Surely, he seems to be suggesting, there are no such causes.

"I mean, I could see her doing something like that if she thought she was righting some wrong, correcting an injustice. Couldn't you?"

"Possibly." The tone suggests that he's losing interest. "Another?" he says, raising his eyebrows in a combination of inquiry and encouragement.

I reach for my wallet.

While he's gone, my own suggestion seems to gain in plausibility. My vigilante daughter, avenger of the powerless. It's something to cling to, for the moment.

When Foley comes back, he reintroduces the subject of Anna. "It was, perhaps, inevitable," he says, and from his perspective, which he begins to articulate at length, this is no doubt true. Foley and an unattached, attractive woman, sharing the same space, unchaperoned – a no-brainer for anyone with a rudimentary knowledge of biology. "In the final analysis it may well turn out to have been meaningless," he says sadly. "If things work out with Emily."

And who is Anna? An artist from the mainland, somewhere in Ontario, Foley reports. Came here a couple of years ago with her sleveen of a Newfoundlander boyfriend, who has since ditched her. Has nevertheless established herself as a member of the local arts community, in fact has a show coming up in the near future at the End of the Planet Gallery, the opening of which Foley hopes I'll be able to attend. Wants me to meet her beforehand. Then I'll perhaps understand if not forgive. Perhaps Maureen – to whom he refers as "your, um, paramour" – could come along.

"Foley, this promises to turn into a sad parody of the ritual of 'meeting the folks.'"

He doesn't get it for a moment, then laughs, shifts in his chair, leans forward, smiles vivaciously: "How've you *been*?"

"Judgmental and condemnatory, apparently. And I don't get it about Velma. This is the twenty-first century. Nobody's called 'Velma.'"

I realize that I've moved the conversation into its mature phase, in the past normally not achieved until after the third pint, a phase characterized by illogical transitions, unintended revelations, a closer-to-the-bone emotional quotient, a general rejection of adult decorum. Begone dull care. Foley will be with me all the way.

It's later, and I hear myself saying, "So Gilhooley takes off his earmuffs and places them carefully on the bar. I'm watching the American and the bartender. They don't say a word. 'Amused disdain' is the phrase. Do you see what I'm saying? Here we are in this super-cool bar on Crescent Street, and Gilhooley walks in wearing earmuffs. It's wasn't a matter of being ironic or defiantly unstylish. He was wearing them to keep his ears warm."

Foley is looking at me with a combination of interest and bemusement. I'm attempting to reveal something of significance, but what? I'm at that point in an evening's drinking when a certain kind of consciousness intrudes, asking such questions as, How did we get here from where we started? Why am I telling this story?

Drinking with Foley has reminded me of the old days with Ray McGuire, when we were perhaps five years younger than Foley is now; I've told Foley this; he's pressed for details of this hitherto unknown dimension of my past life. And now he's getting them. Simple as that?

But why this particular story? I have the sense that I'm supposed to come to a conclusion that underscores some bromide about What's Important for Foley to Know about Life. Ricky Gilhooley has just slammed his grey earmuffs on the bar in a no-doubt-hip little place – is this what they call a "boîte"? – on Crescent Street on an overcast March afternoon in, probably, 1970. He and McGuire and I have driven from Ottawa to Montreal for the day. Have I explained why we've done this? Have I explained who Gilhooley is? (The third roommate in our Sandy Hill apartment, is the short answer – we've all known each other since high school.)

"So then what happened?"

Evidently I've been wool-gathering. Foley is a bit concerned now, waiting for the punchline, the moral, the point of it all.

I'm groping, and then I find it. "Nothing happened. We had a beer and life went on. But I've always remembered that moment. The world, Foley" – and here I move into mock-lecture mode, for we're in the realm where no truth is palatable without irony – "is divided into two kinds of people: those who wear grey earmuffs into Crescent Street bars and those who are contemptuous of those who do. It is important, always, to be on the side of the earmuff-wearers."

Foley glances down at the table. Apparently I've just pounded it with my deformed hand. I wave it at him as we make the connection. "Yes, Foley, you're right. This is my earmuff. Pair of earmuffs. Whatever."

Foley nods sagely, or mock-sagely, playing along. "Next you're going to tell me that we *all* have grey earmuffs."

Actually this hadn't occurred to me. Wouldn't it contradict my theory about the two kinds of people? Maybe not. Maybe it would depend on the circumstances, one man's cool headgear being another man's …

Certainly my reaction at the time was more complex than I've let on. Both the bad guys were Americans, for one thing, a tidbit I've deliberately withheld lest Foley twist the anecdote into an anti-American parable. The bartender's name was Jeff, a guy our age, long blondish hair but neatly trimmed, obviously a draft dodger, not that anyone had problems with that. Bring us your huddled masses of cannon fodder, was the prevailing sentiment. The other one's name was Jake, in his forties, obviously a regular, somehow exuding a sense of being well-heeled. How did that work?

Yes, I was hoping that Gilhooley would notice the amused disdain, would take offence, would speak up in his high-pitched raucous voice that seemed constantly to brim over with anarchic energy. "So, Jeff, first time you've seen earmuffs or what?" Fuck them, these suave

Americans with their amused disdain. But at the same time a part of me wanted to flash a subliminal message to them: Hey, you don't see me with earmuffs, do you?

I won't be passing that on to Foley.

"No, Foley. There are people who do not have grey earmuffs." This is probably false, but it's bad pedagogy to be predictable. Or at least so predictable that Foley could guess correctly.

"You'll excuse me. I must make a phone call."

As he plods off, I wonder how well I've explained what Ricky Gilhooley was all about, and why I thought it appropriate to tell Foley about him.

Gilhooley was an athlete, smallish but wiry, all knees and elbows, neither the size nor the guts for high school football, but an excellent point guard; sandy hair, already threatening to thin; freckles; that chainsaw of a voice. Not much to connect him to Foley there, although Foley did play high school basketball, a pine-riding forward, by his own account, who, when he got into a game at all, was given strict instructions by the coach *not to shoot*.

But women. That's it. Gilhooley's grand passion. The real earmuffs, now that I think of it. Have I made this clear to Foley? Probably not.

Gilhooley and Donna. It was over before he and McGuire and I began sharing the apartment. The breakup was Donna's idea, for reasons never made clear. Gilhooley's devotion to her memory was intense, and made even stronger by the fact that she, a flight attendant with CP Air, was featured in a commercial that ran regularly during prime time. She would be on screen for perhaps a second and a half, saying something inane, projecting a generic blond cuteness.

When Gilhooley saw this, he'd become transfixed, blood draining from his face, eyes getting big, an odd smile appearing. An artist trying to depict St. John of the Cross in one of his major ecstasies could have done worse than work from a photo of Gilhooley's face during those seconds. The commercial over, Gilhooley, still rapt, would sometimes offer a brief reverential comment – "She had the sweetest lips" would be a fair sample – before returning to his normal persona.

Not that he didn't try to start over. But his standard line after a half-hearted date with a new woman would be "Not much there," spoken with a sad shake of the head. St. Ricky of the Earmuffs. Martyr in the cause of love.

I think my reason for telling Foley all this was to impress upon him that back in 1970 it was possible to have such bizarre, naïve, pure obsessions, a phenomenon no doubt completely foreign to his generation of technicians of the flesh. But that point got lost somewhere, probably for the best, since I don't believe it's true anyway. My real motive, I now decide, was to try to make Foley feel bad for not living up to my standards of unhealthy romantic attraction, for failing to worship my daughter. But for all I know, Foley is a Gilhooley waiting to happen, poor bugger.

This is what goes through my mind as I watch Foley make his phone call. Been a while since I've strolled this far down memory lane. I decide that when he comes back to the table I'll change the subject if he doesn't.

Later still, and Anna has joined us, Foley apparently having decided that now is a good time to break the ice, with me at my most friendly and vulnerable. Nothing premeditated – that's not Foley's style – but an opportunity has presented itself to cross a bridge before the toll gates are operating. There's something ominous about the fact that he has for once bought a round, one that includes Anna's morally superior soda water.

Still. Though I've been trying to stay in non-judgmental mode, Anna Walmsley quickly establishes herself as a *bona fide* airhead. She's attractive enough, would have to be to sustain Foley's interest for longer than twenty minutes, although – and this is something he hasn't prepared me for – she's also a serious motor-mouth, capable of committing ever-expanding self-absorbed monologues that end only when Foley interrupts her, loudly. But for much of the time he's content to lean back in his chair and beam at me, as I cringe politely, after a few minutes of tuning in and out arbitrarily, it having become clear that no conversational input from me will be required.

"... came here with Calvin, my boyfriend at the time? He was going to be my life's partner until he discovered he was bisexual. Of course he waits till I'm pregnant to tell me he's got this lover named Adrian, this guy he met when he was drumming for a ballet company at some festival in Vermont. They were sharing a tent or something, which is how they met. Anyway, I'd got pregnant on purpose because Calvin's mother had just died for reasons I won't go into, and I thought if I got pregnant immediately, the baby would be her reincarnation. But then he dumped me and I had the abortion, which was really sad, but what choice did I have? But that was last year and I've got my shit together a lot better now, though sometimes I cry for supposedly no reason.

"… when I'm going out with a guy and I'm walking along the street with him I like to be able to fall against him without telling him I'm going to, knowing he's going to be ready to catch me. Like if he misses me it's a bad sign that he won't catch me in other ways, do you know what I mean? But I haven't tried that with Terry yet, I don't know if he's ready? Or if he ever will be ready?"

This is the first time she's mentioned Foley, I think. I've almost forgotten that he has a first name. His face goes through several changes before it decides that detached amusement is the proper stance. We'll be spectators, he and I, occupants of box seats at the Anna Follies.

"… no woman ever has sex without thinking in her heart of hearts that she wants to conceive a baby whether she's using birth control or not. That's my opinion? A lot of guys can't handle that, they want it to be all about them?" (Though I've tried to keep focused on Anna's face, at this point I turn my head enough to catch Foley's quick wince, only he remains disappointingly poker-faced.)

"… trained to hate their bodies, and refusing to shave anything is one way of rebelling against that? I mean if your body naturally grows hair in certain places, why shouldn't it be there? Calvin actually got off on my leg hair. He liked to take his dick and pull back the foreskin and rub it back and forth on my calves until he came. It was kind of foreplay for him?"

This time I don't dare look at Foley, though oddly I'm starting to like her more now. How can you *not* like someone who tells you this sort of thing twenty minutes after meeting you, as though she's saying, Here's my life, as quickly as I can deliver it; it's yours to contemplate and enjoy.

"... paintings mostly of cod, which is weird in itself since the moratorium happened way before I got here? I've never actually seen a cod, I mean one that wasn't cooked? People do ask about that, me *not being from here* and everything, and I tell them it's the artist's job to intuit what's going on psychically, wherever they happen to be. Even still, I get negative comments. But they're a bit more accepting since I got the Canada Council grant, which happened because Andy Plumno who I went to art school with was on the committee, but I'm not supposed to know that?

"... so the show is called Ghosts of the Cod, right? A lot of it's like what I imagine the spirits of the dead cod would look like. They're kind of hard to describe? I mean, every one is different because I think cod must be as individualistic as we are, so I've given them all different human qualities. Some of them are pretty creepy. There's one that's sort of based on Calvin, like what Calvin would look like if he was a cod ghost, because there was something kind of fish-like about the shape of his face, so it wasn't that much of a stretch? So then I started looking at other people in that light, and it's like, no problem, there are these facial types that you can tell are *Newfoundland* types, maybe because of the centuries of inbreeding ...."

Anna, I'm thinking, is providing an excellent

example of the creative writing class cliché that monologues can end only when interrupted by some external event. Foley has been making throat-clearing noises of increasing volume for some time before he breaks into an awkward speech about how late it is – eleven-thirty is late for Foley? – and how far they must walk to get to the Battery. Amazingly, Anna shuts down immediately, and in thirty seconds we're all shuffling toward the door.

We climb the steps to Duckworth, where Foley solemnly places a hand on each of my shoulders, looks me in the eye with an ironic twinkle intended, I think, to convey the information that putting up with Anna's flakiness has its none-too-subtle compensations. He gives each shoulder a simultaneous pat and says, in a mock-affectedly serious tone, "Be well."

For me it's all uphill from here, but it's warm, and the walk, while it will not exactly "clear" my head, should help to make it somewhat more habitable. Up Church Hill and across the intersection to Long's Hill, three major churches – Anglican, United, Presbyterian – within excommunicating distance of each other, counterpointed by the disreputable Theatre Pharmacy, the two words of its name suggesting what the ecclesiastical establishment is up against. Never mind the presumed fratricide that occurred a few years ago on the street outside, or the dubious medical practice carried on upstairs.

"Does the road wind uphill all the way?" Yes, Ms. Rosetti, in St. John's it usually does. Long's Hill, however, is not that long, especially on this sort of night, when everything seems softened, human-scale, even the *terra incognita* of the dark parking lot to the right, and the impassive all-for-oneness of the row houses to the left.

I drift back to the time when Ray McGuire and Ricky Gilhooley and I were roommates, especially to the thoughts of Gilhooley, with whom I haven't kept in touch, McGuire the catalyst bringing us together. Gilhooley, resurrected tonight in oversimplified form for purposes of my ridiculous parable for Foley's benefit. Grey earmuffs, indeed.

The three of us would listen late at night to CKGM from Montreal, its signal coming in perfectly, bringing news of a parallel universe whose otherness was both attractive and ludicrous.

I remember the British deejay, laid back but somehow intense, occasionally given to quasi-religious declarations – "We play music for your *head*" – often dropping in cryptic scraps of autobiography. After "Season of the Witch," for example, he might say, "That is so much like what's happening in my life right now. I can't begin to tell you. It is so right on. If only you could know. Wow. Now let's get into some King Crimson" – inevitably, the track about the fire-witch coming to the court of the Crimson King.

Then there was the American guy who came on later, even more laid back than the Brit, his soft rap beginning with the play-list: "Chicago, Santana, Pacific Gas & Electric, Al Kooper, Laura Nyro ..." and so on, mock-epic catalogue from a hyper-cool land we'd never visit, nor frankly, would really want to, we with our grey earmuffs.

By now I'm at the impossible intersection of Long's Hill, LeMarchant Road, Freshwater Road, Parade Street, and Harvey Road, a Gordian knot for pedestrians, severable by selective disregard of traffic lights and crosswalks. And isn't the old prof full of classical allusions this drunken evening? Across the clichéd Stygian darkness of the pavement, noting the irony that the new fire station has replaced the burned-down Dominion (is it ten years ago now?) – phoenix-like, of course, as though the fabled bird had decided to reinvent itself in a form that would forestall any future conflagration, having the wherewithal to nip it in the bud or, more accurately, quench it in the spark: a postmodern, wised-up phoenix basking smugly in its excess of self-consciousness. ("Yes, I may be prone to burst into flame, but this will not be a problem for *me*, as opposed to the merely *modern* version of myself.") Along Freshwater, passing the fish-and-chips places, Ches's, Johnny's, Leo's – Odysseus voyaging by periplum (why is Johnny's always empty?) – up the street to the house where no old dog will be waiting, and the newfound, and no doubt temporary, Penelope will no doubt be asleep.

A note on the kitchen table: "Check archived phone message. See you in the morning. Love, M." *Love*. Is this the first time the word has risen between us? I suddenly see it as a fast-growing plant, a huge tulip perhaps, springing up from the kitchen floor, bursting into blossom somewhere above my head, an inverted mauve umbrella. Is the casual deployment of the term innocent or crafty? Surely Maureen is without guile, and I'm experiencing something akin to paranoia, no doubt enhanced by the consumption of alcohol. People use the word all the time without attaching significance to it. It's only normal to do so, and I have no reason to feel threatened. Right?

The message is from Ray McGuire. Give him a call sometime soon. Nothing urgent, but he's found something Cleary-related that he thinks will interest me. It's after midnight here, ten-thirty in Ottawa, too late to call. Of course I could e-mail him (as he could have done me), but that would seem oddly out of keeping with the nature of our friendship, both too new-fangled and too impersonal. If he has something to tell me, I want to hear his voice.

CHAPTER TEN

"Let's blow this popsicle stand," Maureen is saying. She has friends who own a house in a small community round the bay, and they're going to be elsewhere this weekend, so why don't we drive out there? Get away from it all, whatever passes for "it all" at the moment. Maureen has already made the arrangements.

The community is called Wide Harbour, on Conception Bay, just beyond Carbonear, a short drive from the beach at Northern Bay Sands. Nothing much goes on there, Maureen says, which is why her friends like it so much. There's a great view of the bay, in which at this time of year – "August month" – whales may be seen to jump. There are a couple of swimming holes within walking distance. What more, she asks, could one want in a weekend getaway?

"The concept of 'weekend' seems odd to me, since I don't have a real working week just now. Nor do you, for that matter."

In fact, on any given day I'm never entirely certain what Maureen is up to. She has an undisclosed amount of money saved from her mainland job, probably won't be seeking employment until after Labour Day. It's not something we discuss. It's summertime, and why shouldn't the livin' be easy?

"Well, focus on the 'getaway' part then. We leave tomorrow."

The prospect of soldiering on with the writing is bleak. Instead I decide to follow up on Maureen's suggestion that I try to find someone in town with a connection to Cleary. Why haven't I done this before? Is it out of fear that my carefully constructed imaginary version of the man might prove to be bogus? Of course I do have a few biographical facts, but these came via my correspondence with Tom Wetmore, not from any local source. Apparently Cleary was quite forthcoming about the relation between his real-life youth and its depiction in *Sacrament of Ashes*. But Wetmore insisted that he had little sense of Cleary's personality. Someone else in my position would have done more than that.

Of course much is explained by my early training, back in the sixties, when the New Criticism held sway: the words on the page are all that matters, never mind how they got there. And now, four decades later, though much else has changed, my profession continues single-mindedly to trumpet the irrelevance of authorship. Texts are, after all, merely products of political, social, and economic forces. They – and the academic commentator – are what is important, not the writer.

Yet I have this illicit desire to understand the "real" Cleary, the person behind those four imperfect but brilliantly eccentric novels that interest no one else. He goes against the grain in all respects: the "Canadian" novelist who explores ideas entertainingly, the priest who flirts openly with heresy yet remains in the priesthood, and – perhaps strangest of all – the Newfoundlander who hates Newfoundland. And now it seems certain that he's faked his own death. Who *is* this guy?

St. John's is in many ways a small town. It takes me only a few phone calls to track down someone who not only actually knew Cleary in high school, but who was in all probability the closest thing Cleary had to a best friend. Two hours later I'm driving out Thorburn Road to see my old head of department, the man who hired me, Dr. Fabian O'Callahan.

It hadn't occurred to me to make such a connection, but it makes sense. O'Callahan and Cleary, Catholic townies, were born in the same year. Both would probably have gone to high school at Brother Rice. And now that I think of it, O'Callahan has some of the same against-the-grain feistiness that I prize in Cleary. As department head, he introduced a number of new courses designed to promote the development of Newfoundland culture – in theatre, film, journalism, creative writing – over the howls of the many Brits and a few Yanks who had for years imposed their tediously conventional imprint on the curriculum. I can remember Esther Shapiro outlining in her relentless Brooklyn accent the evils of "course proliferation," and Winthrop Crawley wondering aloud in his best imitation Oxbridge (only after a few snifters did the aitches begin to drop) whether it would not be cruelly misleading to encourage Newfoundland students to think that they might produce something that could fairly be called "creative." O'Callahan waded determinedly through this sort of crap and mostly got his way, only to quit a couple of years later under heavy pressure from colleagues such as Shapiro and Crawley, his tolerance for receiving abuse having run out. He retired early.

Now he and his wife live in a house in the woods in St. Philip's, just outside town, where he writes polemical pamphlets on Newfoundland history, literature, politics, culture, you name it – all cogently and passionately written. Every couple of years he publishes the most recent batch in book form with a local press. I see him occasionally at the university when he comes in to do research at the library; he always seems more cheerful than I can recall his ever being when he was head.

"You're working on Phonse Cleary, are you?" he says by way of welcome, never one to beat around the bush. "Thought no one read him but me. Come in, come in. What'll you have? How about a beer? Home-brewed. If you don't like it, tell me. Got ten acres here. Developers want it. Been offered a mint. I tell them to fuck off. I'll show you around later. Sit down, sit down."

I do as instructed. The house is two minutes' walk away from a new subdivision, but you'd never know it by looking out the window. We could be in the middle of a forest, miles from civilization.

"So how did you get interested in Phonse?"

I explain how I came across *Sacrament of Ashes* by accident in a second-hand bookstore downtown, thought it was excellent, and was baffled by the fact that no one I spoke to about it had ever heard of either the novel or its author.

"Not surprising. Not surprising. All anyone knows about from that general era are Percy Janes and Harold

Horwood. Pity. A great pity. Neither one of them could think. And Horwood couldn't write decent fiction. He was a sucker for naïve romantic horseshit. The sixties were made for Harold Horwood. And Janes? Came from a dysfunctional family, so he thought the whole world was dysfunctional, Newfoundland included. Couldn't see beyond his own personal shit. Know what I mean? Seriously depressive personality, projected it onto everyone else. Sad. But Phonse was different. He was smarter. But nobody's heard of him, right? He didn't make it into the new Canadian Library, like Janes, wasn't forever telling the world how great he is, like Horwood, deluded bastard that he is. So there you have it."

He sips his beer, waits for me to say something.

"So you knew him in high school?"

"As well as anyone. Which wasn't necessarily that well. But we had common interests, spent some time together, yes. What do you want to know?"

"What made him tick."

O'Callahan laughs. "Who can say? There's the family background, which you already know about, or so you said." (He's referring to something I mentioned in the phone call setting up the meeting, eager to show him that I'd done some homework, was into this business in a serious way.) "But I don't know if you realize how rare that sort of thing was back then. Not just a mixed marriage, but across class lines as well. Doubly an outsider. My theory is, he tried to rise above it. Did rise above it. Contempt was his weapon, contempt and intelligence. It worked, too. Worked well."

"And you were his friend. How did that work?"

"I was a bit strange, too. Not as extreme, but strange.

Catholic working class, but my father was a Confederate, not common in St. John's. And I was bookish, like Phonse. We'd read stuff on our own, Dostoyevsky, Flaubert, Joyce. That sort of thing. This would be in grade ten, grade eleven. Both of us more independent-minded than the Brothers thought healthy. Nothing overt, no open defiance, none of that. Not two of a kind, exactly. Phonse was always a little more out front, a little more in your face. Politely making a point of showing the Brothers how inferior they were. Interested in mysticism, mystical tradition, too. St. John of the Cross, St. Teresa, that sort of thing. Knew more theology than the Brothers, not that that's saying much. But I didn't follow him there. And I had other friends, a social life, played sports. Phonse wasn't into any of that."

"And then he discovered he had a vocation."

O'Callahan snorts. "Maybe. Maybe. For sure he saw the vocation as a ticket out of here. That was his first goal. 'Shitty little place,' he'd call it. Couldn't get out fast enough. But there was more to it than that. The fascination with mysticism was real. Hard to imagine him delivering homilies, hearing confessions, and so forth – but he managed to avoid that end of it pretty successfully, didn't he?"

"Speaking of shitty little places, isn't it somewhat ironic that he spent so much of his adult life in Ottawa, then?"

"Yes and no. No doubt Ottawa's a shitty little place, too, even more so then than it is now. You'd know about that, wouldn't you? But in a way it didn't really matter where he was going to end up, as long as it was away from here. He would've defeated whatever he hated here by showing himself he could do without it."

"So the vocation thing was fake?"

"Not necessarily. He had ambition, intellectual ambition, and thought maybe that meant he should be in the Church. Not like he had a family to bankroll him so he could go off to Oxford, was it? There weren't too many alternatives for someone in his position."

"But still. Shouldn't he have had some kind of religious experience or something?"

"Not necessarily. It was more like the default option for a certain kind of student. You know, we had sort of a job fair for vocations. Representatives of different orders would come in and set up in the gym, interview students, sort of competing against each other. Of course the Christian Brothers had a big advantage, but there were lots of others, too."

"So why did Cleary make his choice?"

"Partly because he hit it off with the recruiter, closest thing to a kindred spirit. Partly because it was the Oblates of *Mary* Immaculate, probably. Had a thing for the Virgin Mary, Fatima, Lourdes, that sort of thing fascinated him. No doubt because of his mother. You've figured that out from the first novel, have you?"

Yes, of course I have, and the question gives me the opening to discuss my research, leading rather pointedly to the business about "Perdicaris Alive or Raisuli Dead" and the strong possibility that Cleary faked his death.

Does a knowing smirk flicker on O'Callahan's face? "Sort of thing he'd do. Like a joke on the Brothers writ large. Yes, I can see him doing that."

"But there would have been a very good chance that no one would ever get the punchline."

"That's the point about Phonse Cleary," O'Callahan says, placing his empty mug on the table. "He wouldn't care if anyone figured it out. Couldn't give a flying fuck."

Before I leave we go for a short walk in his woods, and then he insists that I taste a tomato from the greenhouse. I'm shocked by how real the flavour is, compared to what I'm used to from the supermarkets. He insists that I take several more. After I thank him, he says, "You'll let me know if you solve the mystery of Phonse Cleary, will you?"

Does the tone imply that he's already solved it? Driving home, I find myself feeling absurdly offended by O'Callahan's characterization of Ottawa as a "shitty little place," though the Ottawa of my youth fits that description. But who is he to say so? On the other hand, I have no trouble endorsing Cleary's condemnation of St. John's, though it was a St. John's I've never known. Which leads me to think of the odd parallels between our lives, Cleary's and mine. He grows up in St. John's and moves to Ottawa. I grow up in Ottawa and – eventually – move to St. John's. My ex-wife moves from St. John's to Ottawa, too. What's with that?

Probably nothing. Can't blame an English prof for trying, though.

Maureen says later, "So you didn't actually ask him if he knows anything about the faked death, if that's what it was. Why on earth not?"

"I thought that if he thought I could be told, he'd volunteer the information. There'd be no point badgering him, anyway. He'd just clam up."

"So what do you know now that you didn't before you went out there?"

"Not much, in terms of hard fact. But I do have a better sense of who Cleary was, now."

"Does it explain anything about his work?"

"Nothing I couldn't have inferred. But it's not so much about his work. I'd just like to know for sure whether he's still alive, and if so, what he's up to."

"Would that knowledge help you to live your life?"

"Probably not."

I go on to explain that I'd really like him to be writing, perhaps publishing under another name. Why would he stop after four novels? I'd like his life now, however weird, to be a principled one, to be one that reflects some authentic change in his own understanding of who he is. What I fear is banality, that he's reinvented himself as an ordinary guy, without illusions or ambitions, drifting comfortably toward oblivion. And why do I fear that?

I remember a conversation I had a few years back with Eddie Laskowski, our resident post-everything-ist. He'd mentioned a well-known art film that he'd almost seen at a couple of different times a decade apart. On both occasions, circumstances had intervened, and he still hadn't seen it. I suggested that this would be a good premise for a story, that the protagonist several times plans to see a certain film, but never quite manages to. (It's an obscure East European or Japanese masterpiece, not available at Blockbuster or the like, so he has to wait for special showings at a university or film society or on a specialized cable channel.) Finally, in old age, he does get to see it, and either (a) its revelatory power is such that it profoundly changes the way he understands his life, though he doesn't regret a moment of it, it's joy all the way, or (b) he realizes with poignant clarity that, if he had seen the film as a young man, he would have lived his life differently, but now, of course, it was far too late to change.

No, Eddie informed me, "You've got the ending wrong. He finally gets to see it – and it's just another film. No big deal, one way or the other."

Dr. Edward Laskowski, incarnation of the *Zeitgeist*.

I don't want Alphonsus Ignatius Cleary to be someone Eddie Laskowski could have imagined.

Wide Harbour is a scattering of houses on a couple of gently sloping hillsides surrounding a harbour that is, well, wide. The fabled Newfoundland genius for devising wackily imaginative place names seems to have come up short here, as is the case with the adjoining communities of King's Point, Williams Head, and Small Cove, all of which blend unobtrusively into one another.

"Who lives here?" I ask Maureen as we pass a small church at the top of a rise, Protestant surely, judging by the arrogantly humble asceticism of its design and location: facing out to sea, no shield of trees or bushes, bland white clapboard thumbing its nose at the elements, no doubt smugly trusting in divine protection.

"Older people mostly," she says. "Get ready to make a left turn as soon as we cross that little bridge."

"I mean, there seems to be no economic activity anywhere along here, apart from the convenience store we just passed and that pathetic-looking grocery."

"Slow down, it's right here. Now, up past the school

bus, past where the horse is grazing, past the Orange Lodge building on the left, and there it'll be, the yellow one. There used to be a fish plant a few miles up the road. A few people work in Carbonear, doing what, I don't know. Some of the men go off and work elsewhere for months at a time – Voisey's Bay, now, some of them. But not that many permanent residents under fifty, Jim and Diane say."

There's a fair amount of space around the house, lots of trees, bushes, unkempt grass, weeds, a general atmosphere of engaging bucolic disorder. While Maureen fiddles with the key, our nearest neighbour, from the ramshackle bungalow on the other side of the narrow unpaved road, peers across at us from his deck. Baseball-capped, long-haired, and beefy, he's far enough away that no acknowledgement of his presence is necessary. Several elderly, oversized cars are parked outside his equally oversized garage. A tethered Rottweiler practices exuberant, snarling leaps to no effect. There's a nice view of the ocean, though – the small bay (or "wide harbour") on the other side of the highway, and beyond it, Conception Bay itself, calm in the sunny afternoon haze.

"We're probably a bit late for the whales," Maureen says, standing beside me. "Should be good blueberry picking, though."

"Excellent," I say, with enough of a Newfoundland twist to indicate mild, friendly sarcasm. "Exlunt."

Later on we drive through narrow, twisting lanes to a parking spot behind the church. Here there's a steep path leading down to an empty, rocky beach where Conception Bay stretches before us.

"Only the locals know about this one," Maureen has explained, "and they hardly ever use it." We're on the back side of one of the small peninsulas that embrace the expanse of Wide Harbour itself. No signs of civilization are apparent from our basking spot.

"We're not skinny-dipping," Maureen says, lest I get the Wrong Idea. "People sometimes do come down here, and it wouldn't be appreciated."

We're in and out in thirty seconds. It's a warm day, the temperature in the mid-twenties, but the sheer inhuman piercing iciness defeats me.

"Hughie, man of the sea," Maureen says, good-humouredly derisive.

She lowers the top part of her unnecessarily matronly one-piece and lies back on her towel. There are some largish rocks between us and the path; I'll be able to warn her should someone approach; it's highly unlikely that anyone will appear on the heights directly above us.

"Can I help you with the sunscreen?"

"Haw. Haw."

Still, it's erotic enough to watch her massaging her (as it seems) unnaturally white breasts. The full breasts of a woman in her fifth decade who has at some point suckled an infant, unpretentiously and innocently declaring something eloquent that can't be translated, something about the poignancy of change and the endurance of beauty. Not a thought that one can express aloud without spoiling the moment. I can tell that she enjoys my looking, though.

Half an hour later we decide to go back to the house.

Later still, when it's cooling off, we go blueberry picking in a miniature valley close by the house. There's a stream and a swimming hole, populated by portly mothers and young children, maybe ten or twelve in all. Two or three glance incuriously in our direction. "A lot of St. John's people have summer places here," Maureen says. "Strangers like us are no big deal."

We move past the swimmers, following a grown-over trail upstream, where Maureen thinks there may be good picking. A hundred yards or so later the valley widens. We walk through what was once a gate in a waist-high fence, most of which no longer exists. We're in deep right field, facing the remnant of a backstop whose weathered wooden frame, here and there festooned by bits of rusted chicken wire, thrusts with sad self-importance toward the not-quite-cloudless sky. It's been a while since it's had to fend off any foul balls, or been able to.

The field itself is covered with weeds, in many places up to our chests. The mound is hardly discernible, a tiny rise in a clump of vegetation. I experience the predictable rush of images – Ozymandias, Wordsworth coming across the old gibbet in the middle of nowhere, ironic reversal of *Field of Dreams*, a pop song called, I think, "There Used to Be a Ballpark Right Here," which I heard on the radio years ago, sung by Sinatra, and even Calvary looming in the background, those tall grey sticks almost in a row.

"This is kind of sad," is what I say. Maureen points out that there probably aren't that many people of ball-playing age around here anymore.

We move on, beyond the backstop, in search of blueberries, our plastic containers at the ready. Maureen has promised to bake a pie when we get back to St. John's.

Sex has become non-verbal, a sacred space we enter as though having taken a vow of silence, Trappists of the flesh. Speech is of course tolerated when necessary, but otherwise it's bad form. Maureen now seems to favour what is known in the current vernacular as "going cowgirl," which is fine with me. We never used to do it this way. Have our bodies changed, or does she want to establish that what happens between us now is new? After the event, neither of us is inclined to talk about it.

I feel grateful – for Maureen's body, for the fact that she wants it to be with mine, for the fact that mine is healthy, for the fact that when it's over we lie there holding hands for a moment, and she smiles at me before we dive into our separate darknesses.

I wake up late, a few minutes after nine. Maureen isn't beside me, but I can hear a radio in the kitchen, and then Maureen making a snorting noise that clearly expresses amused contempt. And then another.

When I get there, she holds up a hand before I can speak.

"Listen to this."

It's the weekend arts program. Anna Walmsley is being interviewed.

"… more, sort of, objective about it?" she's saying. "Because I wasn't here when it happened, I think it gives me a certain freedom. Do you know what I'm saying? To pick up on images that maybe people who've been here all along just can't see?"

"So what are some of these images?" The interviewer's tone is teeth-grittedly neutral.

"I can't believe they're taking this woman seriously," Maureen says quickly. "At first I thought it was a parody."

"… a people literally haunted by the cod. You can see it in their faces, at least I can. I wanted to bring that out in the work."

"The *work*!" Maureen says. "*The* fucking *work*."

"Good morning."

"Listen to her! Hasn't been here more than a year, and she's telling us what we're all about."

"Many people would question …"

"Us?"

"Well, you know what I mean."

"… legitimacy of the vision behind it …"

"What's for breakfast?" I am legitimately hungry.

"Who's to say what's legitimate in art?"

"Wait a minute, I want to listen to this."

"… documenting my feelings about …"

"*Documenting her feelings*? I bet she's never seen a cod that wasn't already cooked."

"Actually, that's true. She said–"

"Shhh."

"… come a long way. I mean when I first came here and people talked about flakes, I thought a flake was like a giant corn flake except made out of fish or something? But then …"

"Agh! Do you believe this?"

Yes. Yes, I do.

CHAPTER ELEVEN

Another hot day, unfolding lazily. We drink coffee on the porch. The Rottweiler neighbour zooms out of his laneway on an ATV and heads down to the highway. His wife, long dark hair, large-breasted, tank-topped, generously bellied, comes out on their deck and starts hanging up laundry. The dog barks. "I'm not in the mood for this," she snaps, loud enough that we can hear her clearly over the barking. No one else is in sight.

The bay is still. It comes almost up to the highway, neatly splitting the town of Wide Harbour in two. To our right, the hill with the church, to our left, the as yet unexplored other half, the one almost a mirror image of the other, both with arbitrarily placed sprinklings of houses on a hill facing the water. Maureen's friends have told her that the people who live off to our left won't necessarily know their neighbours on the opposite side. I suggest that while this wouldn't be unusual in a conventional suburb, it seems to under-cut the myth of the close-knit outport community that so permeates political rhetoric about rural Newfoundland.

"It's all pretty much a crock," Maureen says cheerfully, "the whole business about Newfoundland open-heartedness, generosity of spirit and so on. Years ago I knew someone in sociology doing research on the topic of women from away who marry Newfoundland men and go to live in the man's home community. What she found was that these women were ostracized by the women who'd always lived there. They were seen as having stolen a man that should have belonged to one of them."

"Thank God I'm the one from away."

"Don't worry, I wouldn't try to drag you to a place like this. If we, um, keep on."

"Is there any doubt that we're, um, going to?"

"Don't be flippant."

"Okay. I'll shut up." I feel a bit resentful, as though she's somehow deliberately manoeuvred me into making the first move toward the conversation I've been fearing all weekend that she would instigate. Well, not "fearing," precisely, more like "resignedly waiting for."

"See, that's what I don't want. Talking is good. I want to hear you talk."

"Okay."

"Maybe at somewhat greater length."

"You said that just like I'd say it."

"I'm wondering if that doesn't mean something."

"How so?"

"That we can speak each other's language. So to speak. I mean, if we want to be analytical, what else have we got going, what'll hold us together for the, let's say, medium term?"

"Maybe it'd be better if we didn't want to be analytical."

"I knew you were going to say that, Hughie. And that's just what I'm talking about, sort of."

And so we move through Maureen's studiedly dispassionate checklist of Things That Won't Hold Us Together. Kids – we won't be having any of those. Our misleading mutual interest in literature – I don't like her poetry. She doesn't understand my obsession with Cleary – of course I don't, either. The absurdity of sex as some sort of linchpin, "especially at our ages" – she speaks in the interrogative voice, leaving it to me to deliver the *coup de grâce*: "Who knows when my dick will fall off?"

"So what's left?"

"Well, you crawled under the house for me. That's pretty big. And I'd do the same for you, figuratively speaking. I mean, if there were some equivalent." I would, too, I'm just realizing. Though damned if I can think of an equivalent.

She's quiet for a moment. Then, "I guess that's enough. For now."

At first I think she means that this mutual implied commitment is all we need to keep us going for "the medium term," as she puts it. But a moment later I think perhaps she means simply that we've talked about it enough for now. I decide not to pursue this point.

And if we really do speak each other's language, why am I not sure what she meant?

Meanwhile the church across the way has bonged into life, tangible (well, aural, actually) proof that this is Sunday, different from all other days of the week. The sound of tinny church bells, but surely not real ones. It's a recording – the same program repeated everlastingly. Or could there be some fanatically dedicated *carilloneur* ensconced in the church, steadfastly recycling his half-hour repertoire? I'd prefer it that way, a lone visionary urgently trying to reach everyone within earshot with his gift-wrapped message. But it's clearly the ecclesiastical cognate of Big Brother who's behind it all, who's decided to bombard the countryside with canned oldies from the Christian All-Time Top Forty: *Jesus out of every nation / Has redeemed us by his blood,* but elongated to "Jee-hee-sus ou-out of ev-ry-hee nay-hay-hay-hay-shun / Has re-de-heemed us by-hy his blood."

It's surprisingly catchy, though. Maureen notes that I'm humming it as we pile our stuff in the car, getting ready to drive back to St. John's.

And somehow this leads to her returning to my "obsession" with Cleary. I've suggested that if she wants to talk to me about that, she should read the novels, preferably in order, and in fact she's made her way through *Sacrament of Ashes.* Her verdict: competently written, but she couldn't stand the narcissistic protagonist. (On the other hand, I've noticed that this is a recurring complaint of hers about almost any male-authored novel.) *Isle of the Blessed* is too obvious in its commentary on Newfoundland, and in any case parables aren't for her; she couldn't get through it. And she was put off *Saucers over the Vatican* by its garishly retro fifties sci-fi cover, no doubt inspired by Tom Wetmore's misguided notion of what might attract an unwary reader. No use to explain the disconnect between cover and text, indeed to note that in the text itself there are no flying saucers hovering over the Vatican. She's not interested in UFOs or for that matter appearances of the Virgin Mary, except insofar as they provide raw material for analysis of patriarchal pathology. Which reminds me, I still haven't played Brian Henighan's tape.

So – Maureen suggests as I negotiate the curves on the way back towards Carbonear – maybe I could just *tell* her about the last novel, since she's unlikely ever to read it. And while I'm at it, maybe I could explain why I think it's so wonderful.

Okay, I'll give it a shot.

Cleary's fourth novel is different from the others. There's still the trademark Cleary anti-authority stance, but the cynicism has withered away. What has replaced it is not so easy to describe – an earnestness, perhaps, but one that comes swathed in self-conscious and somehow non-corrosive irony, as though Cleary is presenting his story with an enigmatic smile that invites the reader to resist the impulse to mock.

The Apocryphal Autobiography of Meister Eckhart (1984) is as much a self-portrait as *Sacrament of Ashes*, as Cleary selects and modifies information about the medieval mystic's life and includes, centrally, incidents believed by contemporary scholars to be, as the title acknowledges, apocryphal.

"And who, exactly, was this guy?" Maureen asks. "Historically, I mean."

I've already written my little introductory spiel for this section of the monograph, so I can trot the facts out in a way that Maureen finds suspiciously glib. ("You're not just making this up as you go along, are you?") Eckhart was born in Thuringia about 1260, joined the Dominicans in his teens, studied at Cologne and Paris, held important administrative positions in the order, and became widely known for his teaching and preaching. Accused of heresy in 1326, he was in the process of defending himself (but between trials) when he died at an unknown location sometime in 1327 or 8. He was posthumously condemned for heresy on the basis of seventeen statements made in his writings.

And the nature of his heresy? Basically, that humanity and God are more intimately connected than orthodoxy would allow, that God is real only insofar as He manifests Himself in human consciousness, that indeed God is dependent upon humanity even as humanity is dependent upon God.

"I can see," Maureen remarks, "that saying that could get a guy into trouble in 1326."

"Yes, well, there was more. For Eckhart the story of Christ's birth is the story of God being born in the soul of the individual. And the individual, male or female, then becomes another Christ. The Archbishop of Cologne didn't like that. And it didn't help that he was a Franciscan and Eckhart a Dominican."

"So both sexes can give birth and both sexes can become the Christ child?"

"Spiritually, yes. Proto-feminist, hey? No privileging of masculinity here." I decide not to continue with a disquisition on the Godhead, the fourth and distinctly female member of the Quaternity, the source of all life, human and divine. I don't want Maureen to think that I'm making a crude attempt to convert her into an Eckhart/Cleary fan. That would not be cool.

The Apocryphal Autobiography of Meister Eckhart

begins with a brief prologue supposedly written by Eckhart himself. It comes from a sermon based on the Gospel narrative of the sisters Martha and Mary. The account in Luke contrasts the two: when Jesus comes to visit, Martha runs around performing necessary house-hold duties ("cumbered with much serving" – KJV), while Mary devotes her full attention to what Jesus is saying. Jesus rebukes Martha and praises Mary, saying that Mary has chosen "the one thing needful," namely to listen to him.

Cleary's version of Eckhart perceives irony in this story. It's the "one thing needful," all right, but only for Mary, because Mary is at a lower level of spiritual development than Martha. Martha doesn't *need* to listen to Jesus; she can concentrate on *doing*. In serving others, she's already actively emulating Jesus, not in any mechanical, unconscious way, but because she's already understood that God has been born in her soul, and she's already another Christ. In Cleary's version of Eckhart's sermon, Jesus acknowledges this fact with a nod and a wink, unrecorded by whatever pious scribe happened to be sitting nearby. ·

The main part of the novel is in three sections, each centred on an important event in Eckhart's life that is apocryphal, according to Cleary's short note at the end of the book. The first of these, presented as happening at the time of his first realization that he's capable of mystical experience, focuses on the appearance to Eckhart, "appearance" implying neither hallucination nor visual registration of what is objectively "there," of a naked little boy. Cleary's rendering of Eckhart's account indicates that the boy is in some sense the divine child, the baby Jesus, connecting Eckhart's spirit to eternity. The child becomes a symbol of the purity of his own spirituality as he comes into conflict with Church authority, sustaining him in his effort to change the stultifying tradition he has inherited.

"Good luck with that," Maureen says. "And besides, haven't we heard all too much about Catholic clergymen and naked little boys?"

"It's symbolic, okay?"

"Whatever."

The second section involves Eckhart and his daughter, who, in Cleary's version at least, oddly chooses to define herself as asexual, refusing to conform to conventional gender-specific female roles, claiming an identity that transcends the masculine-feminine dichotomy, though not of course physically, no hermaphroditism implied. The revelation for Eckhart is that he needs to be open to and supportive of his daughter's need to explore her own spirituality in ways as radical as those he has pursued for himself.

"That's you and Emily," says Maureen. "The short haircut, obviously an attempt to de-sexualize herself. And in leaving Foley, she's rejecting a traditional female role, doormat to an oaf."

"A bit of a stretch. She's never been a doormat, for one thing." I have wondered about the hair, though. But I don't say anything about that.

"Is that why you like this book, Hughie? Because you think you're like Eckhart?"

"No."

The third part focuses on one Sister Katerina, who as a young nun is assigned Eckhart as her confessor and spiritual guide. Although she is a presence in the earlier sections, she becomes particularly important near the end, as it becomes evident that she has achieved a level of spirituality far above Eckhart's own. Her key line at the climax of their last dialogue is "Sir, rejoice with me. I have become God."

"Delusional, was she?"

"The point of all this, in the novel, is that Eckhart is perfectly willing to acknowledge her superiority. In no way does it invalidate his own experiences. He has the humility to see what's there."

"So he's delusional too. But humble, so it's all okay."

"You're way too cynical, even by my standards."

This last encounter with Sister Katerina, occurring when Eckhart is fighting the various charges of heresy, actually between trials, sometime in 1327, inspires him to give up the struggle. He recognizes that institutional Christianity can't be changed but knows that Sister Katerina and her ilk will somehow survive, that humanity's connection to the divine will always triumphantly surface, if not in the life of the Church, then in some other form.

So he fakes his own death. (Yes, two novels in a row – it's starting to look like carelessness and/or something Cleary was thinking about a lot.) The accepted version of Eckhart's biography is that he died somewhere between early 1327 and a point in mid-1328 when an official document refers to his demise. In Cleary's world, Eckhart heads off for parts unknown, ready to live out his declining years – he's already in his late sixties – in undescribed obscurity.

The novel ends with Eckhart's enigmatic prayer: "I

pray to God to rid me of God." Cleary's last published line, if you don't count the "Author's Note" that follows.

We've skirted Carbonear, passed through Harbour Grace, and are now barrelling towards the TCH and home. My account of the novel seems to have taken more than half an hour. I don't usually say this much, all at once, unless I'm lecturing. Maureen hasn't dozed off, though.

"So if you look at the whole shape of Cleary's career," she says, "what does it add up to? I mean, what are the common denominators, what's he all about?"

"God and women, not necessarily in that order." I've thought a fair bit about this, of course. But I'm interested in Maureen's take.

"Okay, but more specifically. In his first book he idealizes his mother and runs away from Newfoundland to become a priest, right?"

"Right. So?"

"So what's missing there, Hughie?"

"Probably quite a lot. But what would you say?"

"Well, in most autobiographical first novels, isn't there a first love thing happening, the guy, if the author is a guy, falling in love and losing his virginity and then losing the girl, I mean woman, all that sort of thing?"

"Good point. Cleary skips that entirely."

"Then in the second one, according to what you've told me, the monk has no relationship with women at all, and that prophet missus who comes out of nowhere ends up getting him killed, right?"

"Right."

"And in the third one, I think you said that the Virgin Mary is some sort of special effect created to delude the faithful. No real women involved at all, just a weird patriarchal cartoon version of one."

"Real women need not apply. Right again."

"But this fourth one *is* all about women. According to the way you've described it. And in that last bit with Sister Whatshername, he recognizes that *she's* God. What does that tell you?"

I'm ready for this, since it's the core of my simplistic unifying argument, something that's *de rigueur* for the sort of monograph I'm working on. "He's found a way to connect his two obsessions aesthetically and thematically. And then, the tension between the two having been resolved, he stops writing. He's said all he needs to say."

"Hughie," Maureen says, and there's a light note of mock pity in her tone, "sometimes you are incredibly naïve, for a man of your years. What it *should* tell you is that he finally found some chickie. Mark my words. Your boy finally got laid, big-time."

"At his age?"

"I've heard it's possible."

That evening, back in St. John's. Still nothing from Emily. When the phone rings, I jump up to get it. It's not her, but I recognize the voice, the irritating assertiveness.

"I want to speak to Emily."

"Velma, how you doing? Haven't heard from you for a while." I was hoping for what is sometimes described as "an audible gasp," but what I get is a very brief silence followed by business-as-usual.

"Let me speak to Emily."

"Velma, I've got news. Emily doesn't want to speak to you. Again. Ever."

But the voice is unperturbed. "I don't believe you. Put her on. Now."

Perhaps this is when I should start putting my cards on the table – the Children's Library first, then the newspaper story, then the revelation that Emily herself is the source of this information – in the hope that Velma will reveal more than she wishes to, or anything at all for that matter. But how likely is that? She didn't bat an eye, metaphorically speaking, when I used her name. Instead I say, "What makes you think she's here?"

"You're saying she's not there?"

"Not necessarily."

"This is wasting my time." Click.

I feel angry and unnerved. Who is this woman to be thrusting herself, arrogant and unwelcome, into my daughter's life? Yes, Emily is an adult, and according to Foley entered willingly into an adult friendship with Velma. But some part of me thinks it's my job to protect her from whatever Velma represents.

"Go ahead, tell me I have to 'let go,'" I say to Maureen after sharing the above.

"The important thing is that Emily has let go. Of Velma. If Velma has no idea how to contact her, that's a good sign."

"Yes. Still, I wish *I* was responsible for severing the connection with Velma. 'Severing' as in delivering a roundhouse right to the chin."

"But it's nothing you can control. As you know. All you can do is to be ready if she needs you."

"This reminds me of *American Pastoral*." Maureen

has never heard of it. "A Philip Roth novel. The main character's daughter gets involved in radical politics in the sixties and disappears. For years afterwards, decades in fact, he gets these phone calls from a creepy woman claiming to know where she is, in fact, claiming to be able to contact her. Of course this isn't quite the same thing. But still."

"What happens in the end?"

"The daughter never comes back."

When the phone rings again, ten minutes later, I'm prepared for combat.

"Hey perfesser, is this a bad time? You sound pissed off about something."

It's a relief to listen to Ray McGuire, who seems now to be even more interested than I am in all things Clearyesque. And I'd forgotten to return his phone call before Maureen and I left for Wide Harbour. But he's in mid-flight, rhetorically, before I can begin to apologize.

"… went to another ball game with Moran, and I was saying, So if you're so sure that Cleary is alive, wouldn't he get in touch with any of the priests, is there anybody else? Like somebody who wouldn't feel they had to tell anybody, like somebody in his department at the university, or maybe a student, and he says, Well (you know how he talks), he says, Yeah, geez, there was this one student, ya know, Ray, a grad student, a woman he thought highly of, ya know, which was really rare, and they'd spent a lot of time together, there were even a few rumours, and so I said, Do you remember her name? And he says, Yeah, it was kind of a strange name, ya know, Matilda, something German-sounding, Matilda Magdeburg, I think, something like that, anyway.

"So when I got home I googled her, and it turns out she's a prof at some university in the States, Milwaukee, I think. Got a shitload of publications, too. Anyway, I called her up–"

"You *called her up*, just like that?" (But why am I so surprised?)

McGuire hesitates, then *he* sounds surprised. "Yeah, I told her I was doing research on Cleary, and I was just wondering, there's all this mystery about his disappearance, everybody thinks he's dead, but I'm not so sure. Actually, I sort of pretended I was you."

"And she said?"

"She said, Well, I guess enough time has gone by now that it doesn't matter, but he definitely didn't die in 1985."

"You're not going to tell me that they got together and now they're living happily ever after."

"No, let me finish up here, perfesser. Reading between the lines, I think she sort of felt kind of dumped, ya know. But she didn't come out and say there'd been anything going on, right?"

"Okay, so how does she know he was still alive?"

"Well, two years passed. She's off in the States somewhere, working on her doctorate. She gets a package in the mail, thin, but there's something solid inside. She was really getting into telling this story, right? Like she was reliving something important to her. She doesn't look at the postmark. There's no return address. She pulls the thing out; it's metal, it's flat, it's–"

"A knife?"

"A license plate. And then she remembers. Years before she's told Cleary – they used to go drinking at the

Albion, she told me later, just like us, eh? – she's told him that her father collects license plates from all over the world. And she told him there were several states and provinces he still didn't have one for. There's no note, nothing, but she knows, she just *knows*, that it's got to be from Cleary, his way of saying goodbye. And the plate is from …"

And here McGuire pauses to let me join him: "Newfoundland."

Only he pronounces it, despite my decades-long struggle to correct him, as "New*found*land."

How good it feels to share this moment of minor but authentic joy, separate from our respective anxieties. He's said nothing about his troubles with his son, whose name I've forgotten, and hasn't asked about Emily – and won't.

Of course the elation wears off pretty quickly. So Cleary was here *circa* 1987. My "faked death" theory is now beyond doubt. But – as always – nobody cares. Well, McGuire does of course, but for him it's a hobby, like trainspotting or birding. Professionally I'm at the extreme margin of Canadian academe, working on someone whose work will remain unread, even after my monograph – one shaky rung above *Coles Notes* – is published. It's not as if Cleary is Frederick Philip Grove, the question of whose identity created an ongoing make-work project for the smugly well-funded, though Cleary is a better writer. As are most novelists of the last hundred years.

But Cleary's probably dead by now.

But he is, or was, a good writer. He deserves respect. I'll do what pathetically little I can to see that he gets it. That his name not be lost to the knowledge of men. A good writer. Let me cling to that.

"So you were right," I say to Maureen. "There was a woman. But apparently it didn't amount to much. Maybe even nothing, physically."

"Maybe there was somebody else. Maybe Matilda gave him a taste and he moved on from there. Doesn't that make sense?"

Chapter Twelve

Two days later – still no word from Emily – I'm getting out of the shower when I hear Terry Foley's voice coming from the bedroom. What is he doing there? Can Maureen, who's risen before me, have sent him upstairs to corner me in the *en suite*? But why would he be coming over, unannounced, as this hour (8:20)?

I arrange my towel carefully around my loins. I've long suspected that Foley would like to know how large my penis is, so that he can take comfort in the certain knowledge that his is larger. I will not give him the satisfaction.

But when I step out of the bathroom, I realize it's the radio, Foley on the radio, pontificating about American hypocrisy: "… as of last September tenth, how many American politicians expressed outrage about the fact that Afghan women were forced to wear the *burka*? But suddenly it's a matter of urgent moral necessity for these women to go bare-faced. That same adjective might also, of course, be applied to the slippery prevarications of Bush, Cheney, Rumsfeld, Incorporated – who, despite their strident protestations that their motives are bathed in the radiant glow of altruism …"

And so forth. At the end of it, the local CBC guy says, "This morning's commentary was by Dr. Terry Foley, a Newfoundlander who specializes in Middle Eastern affairs. Dr. Foley will be a regular contributor to *The Morning Show*."

At least he's found a paying gig, however humble. What female producer was he able to charm? Amusing to think of him tucked away in a corner of the capitalist-subsidized beehive, buzzing naively, earnestly, for his tiny paycheque. A cheerful thought to begin the day.

To say that the e-mail is disappointingly terse is to understate: *Dear Dad, Not to worry, I'm still okay and so are the kids. I'm at a friend's place, still in Newfoundland. Don't bother replying to this message. I'll call when I feel up to a conversation. Love, Emily*

Hardly any lines to read between. Why would she need to "feel up to" a conversation with me? I'm at a loss. I don't know my daughter. I know about her only that which I'm equipped to perceive. The complex overview of her life that I've been developing since her childhood is at best fragmentary, at worst, deluded fabrication.

But at least she's safe.

I'm less than a page away from completing the mono-graph, high time, too, as it's the last week of August and the deadline, already extended once, is nigh. Plus, once classes begin it'll be impossible to indulge myself in any pursuit so time-consuming. So I'm staggering toward the finish line, struggling to complete a sentence that begins "Cleary's achievement ..."

What *is* Cleary's achievement, exactly? To have written four novels that interest me and no one else. To have gone against the grain, with wit and intelligence. To have been a Canadian novelist who took ideas seriously. To have been relentlessly ornery and idiosyncratic. To have written novels which could never make it onto a university syllabus (except mine! – but of course they're out of print) because they can't be used to illustrate some grand Canadian theme or other. To have been satirical, in places. To have said exactly what he thought needed saying. To have done it entertainingly.

The temptation is to say all this by presenting contrasting examples from the pseudo-pantheon of current CanLit superstars. But that would be un-Canadian. By the time I've finished the paragraph, the morning has more or less disappeared.

The special meeting of the departmental graduate studies committee comes to order at two o'clock in the seminar room, the walls of which are populated by photographs of Dead White Males – not the ones who wrote the enduring masterpieces of English literature, but those who taught such masterpieces here in days gone by. Most are wearing gowns, an affectation in vogue among the older Brits until, remarkably, *circa* 1990. Them were the days. I recall being taken aside, shortly after being hired, by a senior female colleague, the nuttier-than-thou Charlotte Giles-Broadman. "The Newfoundlander is *stunned*," she confided vehemently. "It is our task to unstun him."

The committee consists of Reg Pike, Barney Power, Nathan Grainger, Eddie Laskowski, and yours truly, the chair: five white males, most of us somewhat alive, depending on the criteria for judgment. None of us wants to be here, either. It's Greg Harkness's fault. Genial procrastinator that he is, he's put off until the very last moment the issue of whether to terminate the career of one of our most inept doctoral candidates on record, one Olivia Oates, who very soon will have completed her ninth year in the program without having produced a dissertation, without, in fact, having produced more than one chapter of a dissertation.

The regulations stipulate that she should have been a goner two years ago. But Harkness caved twice, and now the School of Graduate Studies has put the pressure on: either provide a credible rationale for letting her stay or cut her loose. Like so much in our institution, this decision is the prerogative of the head. But this time Harkness, lame-ducking it, has decided to pass the buck to our committee. My committee.

There's a subtext here, of course. Olivia Oates's supervisor is Alice Plover. For Harkness to make a decision, either way, would be to take sides in the clash of titans: Plover vs. Pike. There's no upside for him there. So the rest of us are here.

Oates is no prize. She was admitted to the program at a time when we were, collectively, so pleased that anyone from the mainland would do a doctorate in our department that no one paid attention to the warning signals now clearly evident in her transcript and letters of reference. ("I have no doubt that, given the necessary support of a dedicated, imaginative, and patient supervisor, Ms. Oates may one day be capable of writing a passable dissertation.") But Oates, whose topic is an unknown – to me, that is – eighteenth-century poet named Philomena Reynolds, is Alice's only doctoral student ever, Alice herself being no prize as a scholar. It took her some eighteen years to be promoted from assistant to associate professor, as far as anyone knows, a departmental record.

I place the file, which we've all read beforehand, in the middle of the table. For a long moment we all stare at it. It's for me to break the silence. "Who wants to begin?"

Pike, briskly: "It's open and shut, isn't it? The woman doesn't belong in a doctoral program. Nine years and there's nothing to show for it. It's a disgrace. A disgrace. Why are we even here? There's nothing to discuss." There's an aggrieved, petulant tone to this speech, which everyone ignores, since Pike always talks this way.

Grainger starts to make noises – it usually takes him a few seconds to warm up – and Laskowski steps into the breech. There's a smooth preppiness to his manner, despite his scholarly commitment to post-everythingism. Completely apolitical, he's our highest profile publisher and will therefore be leaving for the mainland soon enough.

"Thumbs down. This one's a loser. Philomena Reynolds? Give me a break. We're not talking Shakespeare's sister here. This is more like Thomas Gray's granny. Who'd publish this sucker if it did get written? Mas-tur-ba-ti-on-is Press?" Laskowski pronounces "Masturbationis" so that every vowel gets its own syllable. But he's used this one a little too frequently, and no one laughs.

Grainger emits a sort of croaking noise and makes an awkward gesture with his arm to signal that the floor should be his. As chair, I feel compelled to interject. "We're not judging the topic here. It's already been approved by an earlier version of this committee. We're trying to decide whether the student's progress or lack thereof merits termination or reprieve." Nicely stated, I can't help thinking. How even-handed is that?

Grainger finally achieves lift-off. When it comes to self-righteous bullshit, he has no peer in our department. "First," he says, sputtering slightly and moving both arms, unsynchronized, with the unintentional goofiness sometimes evident in those afflicted by the possession of excessively long limbs. "First, I want to deplore the sexism of Eddie's remark. Our profession should be in the vanguard of ..." And here he pauses, apparently not sure exactly what we're supposed to be in the vanguard of; but then the message arrives (telepathy? divine inspiration?) and he moves ahead at full speed. "Of helping women achieve their full intellectual and economic potential. And yet remarks like that, with their crass and demeaning sexual overtones, put us back in the dark ages, back in the days of ..." He waves at the photographs on the wall opposite. "Of the troglodytes who preceded us." He starts the next sentence quickly, to forestall Laskowski's interjection. "I think that ..." And here he holds up his hand in a "stop" gesture while he decides what he thinks. "I think that Ms. Oates has made a very promising start on an ambitious project. *No one* else, as far as we know, has attempted to write about the work of Philomena Reynolds."

He pauses again, allowing Laskowski to interject,

"For good reason." But I'm thinking that Olivia Oates and I may be kindred spirits; perhaps her choice of Reynolds, like mine of Cleary, springs from personal enthusiasm, not careerism. Though probably not.

"Yes," Grainger continues, "Ms. Oates has had her problems. It took her longer than usual to complete her course work, and she failed her comps the first time through. Because she's never had a fellowship, she's had to teach a course or two every semester. There was a bad relationship. There was the time she was hospitalized when she somehow got off her meds. We all know these things."

Actually, we don't all know these things. But no one wants to drive Grainger deeper into the forest of rhetorical overkill.

Laskowski, sitting across the table from him, has begun to mime playing a violin. Pike has been alternating between yawning and chewing on a fingernail, all the while gazing out the window. Power, who has not yet said a word, glares at Laskowski and Pike in turn.

The elephant in the room is the gossip that Grainger and Alice Plover are having an affair. His wife left him two years ago for someone who, she is known to have later confided to friends, is "not completely self-absorbed." Alice's soon-to-be-ex-husband, a stolid biologist, seems more attuned to the world of fins and scales than the one most of us inhabit. She and Grainger are probably waiting decorously to make some public declaration until Alice is officially confirmed as head.

Grainger continues to speak for some time, using words such as "decency," "charity," "the best traditions of our discipline," and so forth. Finally he stops.

"Barney. Your turn."

"I agree with Nathan."

"Do you want to add anything?"

"No."

This is standard procedure for Barney when controversial matters are dealt with in committee meetings. Although occasionally his sense of outrage will get the better of him and he will blurt something ridiculous, he knows that verbally he's no match for Pike or Laskowski, both of whom would take pleasure in making him look foolish, should he attempt to engage them directly.

"So there appears to be no consensus," I say, master of the obvious. "Perhaps if we talked a little more about ..." But after another ten minutes, we come to the sticking point.

"You'll have to break the tie," Pike says.

I've been the perfect moderator throughout. And objective analysis dictates that Ms. Oates should be history. But am I going to say the word that ends someone's career, however pathetic that career is likely to turn out to be?

"I think she should get another year." Much good may it do her.

Grainger claps his hands and grins.

"Why?" It's Pike. He doesn't care, really.

"For the reasons Nathan has been articulating. In fact, Nathan, why don't you write up the memo? I'll sign it and send it on to Greg." Grainger beams.

As we shuffle out, Pike motions me aside.

"Why, really?" He's not hostile, just curious. And though we're not friends, he knows that he has my vote in the headship race.

"Grey earmuffs," I say.

"What?"

"I once saw her wearing grey earmuffs. That's what tipped the balance."

Dumbest thing I've said in my professional life. And wouldn't you know, just as I'm saying it, an image of Olivia Oates pops into my mind: bloated pale face, buck teeth, mousy hair, physically an unfortunate woman, marching in to teach her first-year class, unaware of the big soft grey things clinging, barnacle-like, to the sides of her head.

I walk away before Pike can say anything else.

Power has been waiting for me to finish with Pike. He waves me into his office.

"Close the door. Sit your holy and blessed. You took note of what I said to Pike in that meeting, did you?"

Raissa moves her coffee to one side to allow Aaron Spracklin to unfold a map on the table. "So the premise is," she says, "that downtown St. John's has been, well, pretty much covered, artistically."

"By that she means," Aaron chips in, "that there are references to or depictions of virtually every street, if you include films, fiction, painting, music, poetry, photography, whatever. Any kind of artistic expression."

They're probably right. Even the lane behind the boozecan on Water has been the setting for scenes in at least one film and one novel. For all I know every square inch of downtown St. John's has been rhapsodized over, balladeered about, shot, had its portrait done, been rendered in deathless (or deadly) prose.

"So here's the thing," Raissa continues. "Aaron thinks he's found," ("has found," Aaron interjects), "*thinks* he's found the only street in the downtown that hasn't been, um, treated artistically. So the idea is, we do this film where first we have a sort of guided tour of different streets and we have the actual writers or singers reading or singing or whatever at the location that they used, but then – we'll have maybe a dozen or so, right? – then we'll take them all to this street that has never been used for artistic purposes. We film them sort of wandering up and down the street. And *then* we give them twenty-four hours to create something, something having to do with this street, and we bring them *back* to the street and see what they've got."

Aaron: "See the point? Art can be made out of anything, anywhere. We choose a location simply because no one has yet thought of making art out of it. Then we watch art being made out of it. Art coming into being right before the viewer's eyes. What do you think?"

"Great idea. But where do I come in?"

Raissa: "Well, we hope you won't be offended by this, but we need a guy to sort of focus the storyline on."

Aaron: "A guy who's, well, he has to be a mainlander so that he needs to have stuff explained to him."

Raissa: "And he has to be, well, very literate and well-informed and capable of asking really good questions, and talking about the arts but also, ahh, a bit, sort of, *bewildered*, you know, not stupid or anything but needing maybe more *guidance* than an educated Newfoundlander would."

Aaron: "For example, he'd have to ask directions to

find this street, see, and he'd meet the writers and artists on *their* streets, and he'd get lost a few times, and he'd have to ask stuff like say, who Johnny Burke was, you know?"

Raissa: "I mean we know, at least *I* do, that you know who Johnny Burke was, but you see, a mainlander could credibly be asking who Johnny Burke was, where if a Newfoundlander did it, it would seem fake, right?"

"By 'bewildered' you mean 'stunned,' don't you?"

That shuts them up, but only for a moment. I wave off the chorus of disclaimers. "Okay, I'm flattered that you'd ask, but one question. What street is it?"

Raissa and Aaron look at each other. Aaron hands me the map. "See if you can find it."

I make several guesses. In each case one or both of them can connect the street to something artistic.

"I give up. What is it?"

"See, he doesn't know either. We can't tell you yet. If word got out before we started filming, someone might spoil it by writing a poem or doing a sketch, just for badness."

"We'll have to work fast. Contact the artists, get them organized without telling them about the 'unknown street' aspect of it. They'll all think it's just about *their* street, and then we surprise them by taking them to the secret location."

I tell them I'll think about it. But the "ignorant mainlander" business stings a bit, and I feel a need to retaliate.

"I bet I know about a Newfoundland writer you guys have never heard of." I tell them a bit about Cleary's life.

"A mystery, cool," Raissa says. "What was his name?"

Aaron seems to bristle slightly. There's a strange tension between him and Raissa.

"Alphonsus Cleary."

News to Raissa, but Aaron, though he doesn't bat an eye, stiffens up a bit more and devotes serious attention to his coffee cup.

"What are the titles of some of his books?"

It's clear that Aaron would rather that Raissa hadn't asked this question.

"*Sacrament of Ashes, Isle of the Blessed, Saucers over the Vatican* ..."

"Hey. That's the name of one of your songs."

We both stare at Aaron, who ignores Raissa and speaks directly to me. "I'm in this band, see. The Zulu Tolstoys? We do a lot of social commentary, sort of *faux* hip-hop, right? We call ourselves the Zulu Tolstoys because–"

"You're changing the subject, Aaron. Hugh would know where you got the name, wouldn't you, Dr. Norman?"

"Yes. I would. And I'll be happy to explain. But first I want to know about that song."

"Pretty big coincidence, Aaron. Wouldn't you say?" Raissa is on my side.

"Okay, the song. It's a satire on the sexual abuse scandal here. The idea is that these aliens from space are coming to avenge the victims, since nobody else is interested in seeing justice done. I mean at the level of changing the institution."

Raissa is impatient. "Tell him how it goes."

Aaron looks a bit self-conscious. He lowers his voice

and delivers the lyrics in a barely audible chant:

"Run away, Father, and hide if you can / Saucers flyin over the Vat-i-can /

"Spacemen comin with righteous rage / Gonna nail your ass to a catechism page /

"Aliens comin at you like the Greek furies / Don't need no stinkin judges and juries."

He stops and looks around. "Uh, there's more. But maybe that's enough."

"I think I get the drift. But where did *you* get the title?"

"Yeah, Aaron, and you better tell the truth or it's over between us."

Aaron: "She doesn't mean—"

"No, no, I don't mean *that*. We all know I'm—"

"Happily married," Aaron and I say in spontaneous, mildly chagrined unison.

Simultaneously Raissa flicks her wrist at us in such a way as to draw attention to her wedding ring. "I mean our ongoing multi-project artistic collaboration would be over."

"You must admit," I say, "that it's a major coincidence. Cleary's books were never distributed in Newfoundland. He disappeared almost twenty years ago, and there's evidence that he was here at some point after that. And now you've composed a song titled after one of his nearly nonexistent novels. It's not in any library here, either, and don't tell me that you found it in a second-hand bookstore because I've got standing orders for them to call me if anything by Cleary comes in." A lie, of course, but how would he know?

"Okay, okay," Aaron says finally. "But you have to

promise to say nothing. To anyone."

Raissa and I nod vigorously and make noises of assent.

"I think that I know the person who used to be Cleary. I can't tell you who he is now. I've been sworn to secrecy. And it's only by accident that I made the connection."

"There are no accidents."

We both stare at Raissa.

"Freud said that. Didn't he? Or somebody like that."

We both turn away from Raissa.

"Can you take a message to him?"

"Sure thing."

"Maybe it was Derrida," Raissa adds hopefully.

Late afternoon and Bill Duffett and I are enjoying our last comradely beer of the summer. It's hot and windy in the outdoor area of the student pub, but for some reason the dark, cool inside seems uninviting. Perhaps we're paying unconscious tribute to our former selves of, say, ten years ago, when on a day like this we'd be good for at least four miles despite the sun, maybe even go for a jaunt up Signal Hill. Today we sit at a picnic table and suck on our bottles of Black Horse (him) and Old Stock (me).

"Norman," he says, his habit being to call everyone, male, female, student, colleague, by last name only. "Norman, have you noticed that as they get older, our colleagues have become increasingly delusional?"

Before we finish the first bottle we've identified and discussed several examples of this phenomenon. Skilled as readers of texts, our colleagues, we conclude, are by and large incapable of making the most obvious rational inferences about real-life situations.

"Of course," Duffett says, "our colleagues are probably making similar comments about us as we speak."

"Except Stiggins." No one in the department will socialize with him.

"And Power." He refuses to socialize with anyone in the department.

"Power," Duffett repeats meditatively. "The fifth Irish Beatle." There's history here. Some twenty years ago, when Duffett and his wife adopted their son, Barney Power took it upon himself to inform Duffett that adopted children were likely to have troubled lives, no matter how dedicated the adoptive parents were. I can picture Barney doing this – well-meaning, pompous, totally insensitive, intending only to make it clear that he thought that Duffett should not blame himself if things did not turn out well, but instead inspiring the sort of long-term low-key anger that is sometimes described as "smouldering."

"Power," Duffett says again. Many negative comments could follow, but he, unlike me, can't bring himself to make any of them. "My round," he says, rising.

When he comes back, he starts telling stories about his boyhood in a small community on the South Coast. "It was medieval," he says. "A bell would ring and everyone would stop work and go in for lunch. Like peasants. There was no money. I mean literally no one had any cash. This was the fifties."

He talks about his grandfather, a highly respected

man. One day a visitor to the fish plant slipped on the slick floor and instinctively reached for the nearest object, which happened to be a machine with unshielded razor-sharp blades, severing three fingers of his right hand just below the knuckle. Someone managed to catch the fingers before they hit the floor. At this point in the telling, Duffett glances briefly, no doubt inadvertently, at my own imperfect hand. Duffett's grandfather calmly asked everyone not to move, and walked out of the plant and into the woods. It never occurred to anyone not to obey him. The visitor, in shock, didn't budge either. Fifteen minutes later he came back with a handful of what Duffett calls "spruce bladder," the gummy substance that oozes out of the bark. "Used it to glue the fingers back on," he says. "It worked, too. A year later the guy came back again, and his hand was fully functional."

Home again, and Maureen's not there. A note on the kitchen table. Not another one, I'm thinking as I grab it. But no, it isn't. Maureen is reminding me that she's gone out to dinner with some female friends this evening. At such moments it strikes me that there's a whole other side to her life that I haven't yet penetrated, a world of close connections with people who are, at this stage, merely names, the actors in little anecdotes that Maureen will tell me when she's in the mood. I've met some of them in person, but usually only for brief conversational exchanges. All this will change, Maureen assures me. She's certain they'll like me, eventually.

I'm about to take a pizza out of the freezer when the

doorbell rings. It's Brian Henighan. He's surprised that I'm surprised. We made an appointment, he tells me, to watch that tape he told me about. We have? I suppose it's possible, though I have no recollection.

"Must be early Alzheimer's," I say with calculated self-deprecation. Haven't I used that line recently? Can't recall.

Brian nods gravely, as though early Alzheimer's may indeed provide a plausible explanation. He accepts the offer of a beer, good Catholic boy, no trace of the puritan. Here we are, two guys enjoying a late summer evening *chez* Norman: beer and the Virgin Mary. We watch in absolute silence.

Mary's Miraculous Medal is a documentary composed entirely of stills. Voice-over is by a man with a faint but discernible Irish accent. St. Catherine Labouré was born in 1806 in a small village south of Paris. Shortly after her mother's untimely death, she dedicates herself to Mary. As a teenager she has a dream about a priest, who, when she later sees his portrait, turns out to have been St. Vincent de Paul. In her early twenties she joins his order, the Sisters of Charity, in Paris. On a July evening in 1830, Catherine is awakened by a mysterious child of four or five, whom she later takes to have been her guardian angel. The child leads Catherine to the convent chapel, and there's Our Lady Herself, sitting on the very chair I'm looking at in a photo right now. Catherine communes with Our Lady, as depicted in various paintings and sculptures, for several hours. When it's over, she comes away with two things: the design of the medal (which must be "properly blessed" to become effective), and the formula to be used in intercessory prayer: "O Mary conceived without sin, pray for us who have recourse to thee."

Predictably, she at first has difficulty convincing her spiritual director that what she experienced was real. But the concept of the medal is so strikingly original and theologically sound that someone begins mass-producing them, and they immediately become associated with a variety of apparently miraculous cures and conversions. The Archbishop of Paris gets into the act and appoints a commission to investigate. In 1836 it declares that Catherine's experience was "of supernatural origin."

Catherine meanwhile remains anonymous. She has told no one but her spiritual director. As the fame of the medal spreads, it becomes known only that an unidentified Sister of Charity is responsible for its creation. As early as 1835, a million of them have been cranked out. The narrative starts to turn a little sour. A certain degree of triumphalist crowing is evident in the report that the medal is responsible for the conversion of "a wealthy French Jew," to say nothing of Cardinal (as he was to become) Newman, who ditches the C of E within two months of his having begun to wear it.

But wouldn't he have been pretty close to conversion to be ready to wear a Catholic medal in the first place? I think about sharing this thought with Brian, but don't want to risk puncturing our little bubble of fellowship.

Soon a cynical subtext begins to suggest itself. The "conceived without sin" business provides support for the movement to accept the doctrine of the Immaculate Conception. Then in 1868 Lourdes happens, upstaging Catherine but giving Pius the Ninth more pro-Mary ammunition. Catherine dies in 1876, her identity never having been revealed publicly. Her body is exhumed in 1933 and found to be "in a perfect state of preservation." Pius the Twelfth would later call her "the saint of silence."

It's easy to say what Cleary would say, what Maureen would say. To mock – or lament – the quality of a spirituality that relies not on direct contact with the divine but instead with physical contact with a metal object over which certain words have been said by a properly qualified person, a metal object whose characteristics were revealed to a young woman not by a divine being but by the apparition of a former human being (not technically deceased, I believe) who has privileged access to the divine.

When it's over, Brian says, "I don't expect you to say anything. I'm glad you took the time to watch it with me, though."

I'm afraid he's going to ask about the medal he gave me, but he doesn't. (It's lying at the bottom of the bowl of loose change I keep on my dresser.) Instead he asks about my family, so I tell him about the Emily-Velma enigma. Why not? Neither Raissa nor Foley has been any use.

"You know what that reminds me of? That Coleridge poem about the girl in the forest."

"*Christabel*?"

"That's the one. From what you've described, that's what it sounds like."

I remember the *Christabel* class, Brian noting for the benefit of his bored younger colleagues that the narrative illustrated a sound Christian principle, that Christabel carrying Gertrude across the threshold of the castle shows that evil must be invited into one's heart, that its power lies in its ability to deceive and seduce, to obtain the co-operation of its victims.

"So you think Velma's goal is what – to destroy Emily's soul?"

"I do. That's how Satan works."

"That's pretty heavy, Brian."

"I know. But I've learned to trust my ability to know the truth. I've got what's called the gift of discernment."

After he's gone, I think of Catherine struggling to convince her spiritual director that her experience wasn't "just her imagination," her lifelong anonymity as she worked in a hospice for the sick and the old. And then I think of Brian taking care of his autistic son, about whom I've forgotten until this moment.

Chapter Thirteen

Dear Dad, the email begins, *I guess I owe you an explanation. I'll try my best.*

I scroll down. There's a lot of text. Brace yourself, Norman. Here it comes.

I'm still here in Newfoundland, somewhere around the bay. The kids are having a great time, but we'll be leaving next week. For Ottawa, not Vancouver. I've been in touch with Mum, and she and Keith have agreed to help us get on our feet there. I need a fresh start.

I think now that I never really intended to stay in St. John's. I did want to see you. And for the kids to see you. I also wanted to tell you about the situation I got myself into in Vancouver, but I couldn't. Why, I don't know exactly. Partly because I thought you might be judgmental, I guess. Plus the fact that the whole business doesn't make much sense.

(Judgmental? How unfair. When have I ever been judgmental with her, except in the case of Foley and then only mutedly and, it must be said, rightfully so?)

(It has nothing to do with Terry, but you've probably figured that out. Yes, he's a slimeball and I'm better off without him, but I've known that for a while.)

This is the hard part, explaining what can't be explained. How one person gets to have power over another. There was this woman I became friends with, Velma. There was something special about her, or so I thought, something charismatic, something that made me want her to like me. And she convinced me that she had – and this will sound really silly – that she had by accident discovered the identity of a serial killer, who happened to be from St. John's, too.

Far-fetched, right? But here's the thing. There are three cases of unexplained disappearances in St. John's, going back twenty years and more. I mean women who simply vanished under suspicious circumstances, possibly murdered, but no bodies ever found. That much is factual. You can check it out for yourself.

In December 1978, a seventeen-year-old girl was given a ride by two brothers from Kenmount Road to Long's Hill, where she lived in a boarding house. They let her out, saw her speak to a man on the sidewalk, then run down Long's Hill. She was never seen again. In December 1982, a twenty-five-year-old woman walked out of a downtown bar, leaving her purse behind with friends, saying she'd return soon. She never came back and hasn't been seen since. In November 1984, a twenty-year-old prostitute left another bar, asking a friend to hold on to her wallet, saying she'd be back in twenty minutes. She was seen getting into a car in front of the War Memorial, and that was the last time anyone saw her.

Velma said she heard about these cases from her crazy Newfoundlander drug dealer then-boyfriend, who claimed to have murdered all three. It wasn't boasting, exactly, she said. It was more matter-of-fact than that. And he seemed to have a lot of information that, as far as Velma could tell, wasn't on the public record. Why would he tell her that, she asked him. She could turn him into the police. Good luck, the boyfriend said. The police know about it. I've given them some help in the past. They're not going to do anything. And after they broke up – for unrelated reasons, Velma said – she did try contacting the police in Newfoundland, and got nowhere. They just told her to get lost, basically, that it was none of her business, she was delusional, possibly angry about the break-up and seeking revenge, that sort of thing.

So Velma recruited me to perform this act of vigilante justice. I was the first person from Newfoundland she'd met since her boyfriend, she said, and the thought that I could have been his victim too, since I was in St. John's at the same time as he was, made her decide that it was time to act. She was very persuasive.

So she got me to do something stupid and evil. As soon as it was over, I understood it for what it was. And I had to get away. I couldn't make a clean break from her – even after it happened I felt deeply connected to her – so I told her I was going home because of Foley cheating on me but that we could stay in touch.

That's it in a nutshell. As far as what actually happened goes – Well, you've seen the newspaper clipping.

I'm almost ready to talk to you. But not yet. And please don't reply to this. I'll call. Maybe later today, or tonight.

Love,
Emily

My first response is: she's made it all up. Yes, Velma exists (objective evidence from Foley) and yes, she is probably the woman on the other end of the phone calls (afflicted by an unfortunate telephone manner; maybe she just has problems of her own that Emily has been trying to help her with but has now had enough of) and yes, the event recorded in the clipping no doubt occurred (but probably didn't involve either Emily or Velma). My conviction that Emily is a criminal has been replaced by the more certain conviction that Emily is a liar. Happy days!

Perhaps this is what Brian means by "discernment."

And what makes me so sure?

I think of Bill Duffett's Chinese student and the elaborate fabrications in her letters home. I think of Cleary's cryptic note left in his van, a tease for those who couldn't give a good goddamn about the truth underlying it – leaving that up to me, for whom said truth is a tiny trophy on the mantelpiece of my professional ego.

I can ferret out the truth in art but not, apparently, in life. At least not my daughter's life. The narrative she's probably trying to deliver is too subtle for me to tune into.

I think of the young woman in Raissa's film, struggling to make herself understood.

I will never know Emily's true story. And I have no idea why she wants me to believe this one. I must grant her the freedom to choose her own artistic premises, I will not challenge her.

Geraldine is Christabel's ghost or projection. But of course Christabel, as dozens of state-of-the-art scholars have no doubt said, "produces herself."

I turned away from her when she was nineteen and needed to be with me or thought she did. Maybe I'm the guy who deserves to be nailed in a hit-and-run. Justice, judgment. The story is about the judgment of the anonymous man projected onto and reflected back from that two-dimensional figure called Velma.

Did she think I was being "judgmental" when I rejected her? But it wasn't about her. It was about me! And haven't I earned forgiveness by being willing to take her in now? Was the real purpose of her visit to test me on that point?

First I tell her she can't live with me. Then she takes Foley from me in some kind of bizarrely misguided act of revenge. Ten years and two kids later, Foley rejects her, implicitly, by screwing around. So she comes back to see if I'm any better than he is, if I've become human at last.

Or am I missing the point yet again?

"Hellew."

"Foley."

"Hugh. Me buddy."

"Emily emailed."

"And?"

"She's fine. The kids are fine. She's somewhere around the bay with an anonymous friend. But she's moving to Ottawa next week."

"I see."

"I don't know much more than that. She said she'd call, maybe later today."

"Well then. There it is."

"There it is indeed, Foley."

"I have of course been attempting to communicate with her myself. She has not so far deigned to reply."

"You're on your own there, Foley."

"That I know too well. The vagaries of the female mind." He pauses, inviting me to contemplate the profundity of this observation. "Speaking of which, there's a matter I'd like to discuss with you, perhaps over cups."

"Over cups?"

"I'm sure you catch my drift, as the cliché has it."

"I'm not sure I want to catch anything from you, Foley. Is this going to be about your bird?"

"Ah, if only it were that simple. No, this is not about my bird."

"Foley, tell me. How often in your life have you been able to make that statement truthfully?"

"Witty as ever. What about the Ship, around two? I'll buy the first round. I have a paying gig, of sorts."

"I heard."

Five minutes later, the phone rings again.

"Dr. Norman?"

"Yes."

"This is Aaron Spracklin. How are you today?"

"That question does not admit of an easy answer, Aaron. Let's move on. Is this about the film project?"

"No, it's not. It's about that gentleman whose literary career you're interested in."

"Yes?"

"He may or may not meet with you. Tonight. The Duke. At eight."

"How will I know who he is?"

"He'll know you."

Running again. Cemetery to the right, then the Pen, the Lakeside Hotel. Focus on the time, the purity of those numbers. Past the building on the left, the boathouse or whatever they call it, onto the footpath. Emily will explain all. Then I'll meet Cleary. My mini-quest at an end. Apocalyptic denouement.

But for now I'm in my run-bubble, separate and apart from the world around me. Where's my elderly acquaintance of colour, he who walks (or used to) around the lake clockwise? Confirming our separate separatenesses with meaningless greetings. If we'd ever stopped to chat, what mutual disillusionment, no doubt. Both of us would be angry after the fact at having our respective rhythms interrupted. Focus on the watch. Time ticking away. Go for the personal best, though it won't be. Gotta get back to the cemetery, quickest.

The Ship at two. The lunchtime crowd of hard-drinking lawyers has pretty much cleared out. Foley sits at a table in the back corner, peering down at his pint, a disconsolate look to the posture. When I haul out my chair, he smiles up at me, but only perfunctorily. "I'll," he says, gesturing towards the bar and then stopping as though in hope that I might spring up and insist on buying my own. Instead I sit, lean back, and grin engagingly.

"I come from haunts / Of coot and hearn," I tell him.

"Whaa?" He thinks it might be a joke, but he's not sure.

"I make a sudden sally." I gesture toward the bar, cruelly dispelling his uncertainty. "Smithwicks. Tennyson going through my head. 'Da-dah da-*dah* da-dah da-dah / Dee-dee, de-*doo*-doo valley.' Can't get it out of my head. Don't you hate it when that happens?"

He shuffles off to the bar, puzzled. I haven't realized until now what a good mood I'm in. Burdens are lifting, somehow. Maureen and I seem to be on solid ground. Emily and the youngsters are safe and well, and she's committed herself to speaking with me. And I've reconciled myself to the fact that her life will remain shrouded in mystery, as they say. Finally, I've finished the Cleary project and tonight I'll finally meet him. In a week's time I'll be making an amusing spectacle of myself, talking about books in front of fifty or so students, many of them suffering from incurable bored indifference – but there are more painful ways of making a living.

Of course at the moment there's Foley.

"Things are not working out, I fear."

"Pity." I pronounce the word in as Foleyesque a tone as possible, but he doesn't seem to notice. He has a message to deliver.

"It began … Are you listening? You seem a bit distracted."

"I'll try to focus. It's your nickel, after all."

"The irony that our positions have reversed is not lost on me, I assure you. It started with sex. Post-sex, actually. She can't bear to be touched after having sex. It was hard for me not to take this personally. As you might imagine. Most women enjoy a bit of post-coital cuddling, as I'm sure you've noticed. Over the years. And of course it makes for a convenient natural transition to the next, er, conjunction. So I tried to reason with her. Didn't work. Never bothered other men, she said, so what was my problem. Calvin, for example. I've been hearing rather a lot about Calvin the last couple of days. After she'd had sex with Calvin, he couldn't get out of bed fast enough. When I pointed out that he probably wanted to go off and fantasize about boys, that didn't go over well, either. Then ... you recall that evening of debauchery when I introduced you?"

"The Night of the Grey Earmuffs?"

"The what? Oh. Yes. Right. Remember what she said about wanting a man she could fall against without warning, in the certain knowledge he would always catch her?"

"Vividly."

"As of yesterday, I have been officially declared an unreliable catcher."

"How unfortunate."

"There's more. I have rapist tendencies, she thinks. Pressed for evidence, she appeals to her intuition. Unspoken, of course, is that fact that my libido is somewhat stronger than hers. And even that's not everything. I would be an unfit father for her child. Who said anything about a child? I already have children, I told her. We've been together what, a week? Not much more, anyway."

"I have the feeling that you're building, very gradually, toward some grand conclusion here."

"Then the proverbial last straw. I made an injudicious remark about the quality of her work. And the appropriateness of her subject matter, given that she's not, well, *from* here. I had no idea her ego was so fragile."

"The 'last' straw?"

"As of five this afternoon, I'm required to vacate the premises."

"Bummer." I know what's coming.

"I think you know what's coming. I was wondering if–"

"No."

"I see."

I've betrayed him.

"You know, my fellowship money hasn't quite run out yet. And they're giving me $150 for each of these radio commentaries. And the local print media, both tabloid and broadsheet, have not been unreceptive to a couple of proposals. I could make some contribution …"

"Foley, you don't see it now, but I wouldn't be doing you a favour. Believe me."

"I don't doubt your good intentions, but it's true I don't see it now. It would of course only be a temporary …" The prodigal ex-son-in-law. I'm tempted, but only for a moment.

"It would start *out* as temporary. But it might turn into something else. And that wouldn't be good. For anybody. Look, I have to leave. Have another pint. On me." I deposit a five-dollar bill on the table with what I intend to be a "flourish" and start moving toward the door, leaving most of my own pint behind. As I step toward the door, I ask him to keep in touch. As if he needed to be asked.

He gives me a sad little wave to indicate that he's heard.

I can't help but chuckle as I climb the steps up to

Duckworth. Is this the first time I've refused to give Foley what he wanted from me? Whether or not, it was the right thing to have done. For his own good. And mine of course. If I showed up with Foley as surprise houseguest, how would that go over with Maureen? Not well, I'm guessing, and she'd be absolutely right. If I were her, I'd leave me. And I don't want that.

The call from Emily is low-key. There are no surprises. She briefly reiterates the story she's told in the email. The tone is rueful, self-deprecating. Silly her, she says. To be taken in like that. Hoodwinked. Hornswoggled. She giggles at the silliness of the words. Perhaps the speaking aloud is cathartic for her. She doesn't mention my judgmental nature. I listen respectfully, not challenging her on any point. There's a warmth in her voice that I wasn't expecting. It fills me with hope. How naïve must I still be.

Only once do I try to take control of the conversation. "There's something you need to tell me."

"Yes?"

"The hit-and-run. Were you the driver or the other one?"

"Dad." Reproach, or an adult calming a child.

"Yes?"

"What do you think?"

"It couldn't have been you, driving."

"I'm glad you think that."

"And?"

"And nothing. Please just go on believing that. Whatever I said could be a lie, anyway."

I call Raissa to tell her about Emily. It has occurred to her too, that Emily may have made everything up. Or so she now says.

"But why?"

"'The heart has reasons the head cannot understand.'"

"What?"

"A quote you gave us in class once."

"Oh. It's Pascal."

"Whoever."

As often happens with Raissa, the conversation moves on to other topics. I tell her about the meeting with Cleary.

"Is Aaron going to be there?"

"I don't think so."

"Good. Listen," she says, suddenly excited. "Would you mind if I filmed it?"

"What?"

"I'd be very discreet. I'd be off in a corner somewhere. You'd hardly notice me."

This is difficult to believe. Hardly being noticed is not Raissa's style. "But why?"

"I'm sure I'll be able to use it somehow. I see it as a sort of *film noir* thing, these two guys who've never met before but there's this strong connection between them, so there'll be all sorts of tension, really interesting facial expressions and body language, minimalist dialogue with every word having depths of meaning, with maybe the potential for violence hinted at somehow."

"What?"

"I'm not saying there would *be* violence, just the idea

that it *might* happen."

"No."

"No what? No violence?"

"No filming."

"But didn't you tell us that *everything* is fair game for art to make use of? No subject matter is taboo, and stuff like that?"

"That was then. If you try to film us, there *will* be violence. Directed at you."

"All right, I give up. There goes your last chance to have sex with me, though."

"I know you're joking because you're ..." And here I pause, no need for either of us to deliver the perennial punchline.

The Duke at five to eight. Almost empty, too early for the crowd. A woman sits at a VLT, two older guys (that is, in my general age range) are playing at the lone pool table, three younger guys engage the bartender in guffaw-punctuated chitchat, no one in the small outdoor area. I go up to the bar to collect my pint.

I sit at a table in the corner farthest from the bar, where I can see the door and, incidentally, a large-screen TV tuned to a sports channel, blessedly muted. But there's no game on – it's too early for the Jays – and I get engrossed in a highlight reel of this year's Super Bowl, Patriots and the heavily favoured Rams, David and Goliath, the Pats with their out-of-nowhere rookie quarterback Tom Brady, a miracle they've made it this far. What a great myth to buy into, the marvellous boy hauling the sword out of the stone, the stuff of the juvenile sports novels for ten-year-olds.

I watch the Pats' final drive, game tied, under a minute left in regulation. Though I can't hear him, I know the dumbass know-it-all commentator is saying, "I don't agree with *this*," offended that they'd be so confident as to try to score instead of running out the clock and taking their chances in overtime. A last completion, Brady to the tight end Jermaine Wiggins, an obscure journeyman making the most of the limelight (and already dumped by the Pats during the off-season). Seven seconds left, as Brady spikes the ball to stop the clock. And then, as time runs out, Adam Vinatieri boots the field goal for the win.

I realize I'm not alone.

But it's not Cleary, it's Aaron Spracklin.

"Great finish, wasn't it?" he says.

"A storybook ending. But where is he?"

"May I sit down?"

I gesture at the chair opposite me. "Feel free."

"He decided he couldn't come. Said it wouldn't be appropriate. He said he wasn't afraid you'd blow his cover or anything like that. He says nobody would care at this point. But he thinks it better that you know him only through his work. So he sent me instead."

"Why you?"

"I think he sees me as a sort of kindred spirit, maybe even a surrogate son. Something like that. Think of me as his press secretary. And you're the press. And please don't look so disappointed. I can answer questions on his behalf."

"This is ridiculous."

Aaron looks hurt. "Well, it's me or nobody," he says,

but not as belligerently as he probably intended. But how did he expect me to react? Press secretary indeed. No doubt seeing himself as aggrandized by his association with Cleary's ...what? Greatness? No. Charisma? Charm? Whatever. (But isn't my work on his novels analogous to that of a press secretary, except that I provide answers to questions that haven't yet been asked?)

"Lighten up, Aaron. I'm not in the habit of shooting messengers." Raissa thinks highly of him, I remember. And he has Cleary's confidence. He must have something.

"Just ask me a question, Dr. Norman. I can't tell you who he is now, anything that might identify him. But everything else is fair game. I know him pretty well."

"Do you? And how did that happen?"

"Well, apparently he was impressed by my work. He approached me at a cast party after a play at the Hall, told me so then. Of course I didn't know who he was, I mean who he used to be. He's somebody else now. Anyway, we hit it off. Had me over to his house, we talked about what's going on here artistically, asked me about my plans, ambitions, that sort of thing. Then he gave me a novel by somebody called Cleary. *Sacrament of Ashes.* Told me to take it home, read it, tell him what I thought. I was hooked, thought it was great. When I brought it back, he told me. Gave me the others. Swore me to secrecy but said he wanted someone in the arts community to know what he'd done. Picked me, he said, because of my promise. We meet regularly, to chat. He's a good guy. That's about it."

"So how much has he told you about his previous

existence, and why he came back?"

"A fair bit. What do you want to know?"

"Who else here knows about him?"

"Not many. A few people he could trust. That O'Callahan guy retired from the university is one. He phoned the other day, apparently, mentioned you were interested in the novels. I don't know all of them."

"And why did he do it? Fake his death? Quit the priesthood? Come back here? What's that all about?"

"Okay, he knew you'd ask that. So he told me to remind you about the prologue to the Eckhart novel, the sermon about Martha and Mary. He said, and this is a direct quote, that for his whole life he'd been Mary and it was the right time to become Martha. Does that make sense?"

"Okay, that would explain leaving the priesthood, but why the faked death?"

"He said to tell you first that it was just for badness. Which he says it was, partly. Also he didn't want the bureaucratic hassle of leaving formally. But mainly he wanted a clean break between his old life and his new one. I guess he got it."

"Pretty much. But why come back here, if he hated the place so much?"

"Just because he did hate it. If his former self hated it, his new self would have to learn not to hate it. It was a test, he said."

"And how has that worked out?"

"Well, I think. But I can't go into detail."

"Does he still write? Publish under another name maybe?"

"See, that's the sort of question I'm not allowed to answer. Just like I can't tell you whether he's married or not, whether he has kids, whether he's straight or gay, whether he has a regular job, how he makes his living. He said all of that is irrelevant to an understanding of the novels you're writing about. He said to tell you that the person who wrote them said all he needed to say. Regard that person as dead, he said."

"So I'll never get to meet him?"

"Who knows? Maybe you already have."

"Did he say that?"

"No."

And that's all I can get out of him. A few more people have come into the bar. The Jays are on the TV. In a couple of hours downtown Friday night will begin in earnest. Aaron shifts the conversation to the film project he and Raissa have cooked up. They both hope I'll be part of it. And no, Cleary – or perhaps "post-Cleary" – will not be involved. Nice try, though.

He leaves shortly after. So much for the grand climax to my quest for Cleary. I finish my pint, staring, for some reason, at my deformed fingers. No storybook ending there, either, the pinky still caught in the act of trying to escape from its Siamese non-twin. I walk out into the warm evening.

We're going out, Maureen and I. She wants me to meet some people. But first she wants to trim my beard, which she says is a bit scraggly.

"The very word that Emily used. But then I had it trimmed at The Family Barber."

"And how long ago was that?"

I sit obediently, swaddled in a spare tablecloth, red and white checks. She plugs the shaver in, peers calmly into my face at close quarters. God knows what she sees there.

"Hey there, Martha," I say, knowing she won't get it. But I'll explain everything later.

Acknowledgements

First readers: Claire Wilkshire, Lisa Moore, Michael Winter

Those who comprised a warm and insightful audience during the early stages of this book's evolution: Libby Creelman, Ramona Dearing, Jack Eastwood, Mark Ferguson, Jessica Grant, Mike Jones, Mary Lewis, Lisa Moore, Beth Ryan, Martha Wells, Claire Wilkshire

Editor: Annamarie Beckel

Designer: Rhonda Molloy

Also at Breakwater: Chad Pelley

The material in Chapter Eight on the comparison between the event at Fatima and UFO sightings is taken from Jacques Vallee, *The Invisible College* (New York: E. P. Dutton, 1975). The material in Chapter Eleven on Meister Eckhart is taken from John P. Dourley, *A Strategy for a Loss of Faith: Jung's Proposal* (Toronto: Inner City Books, 1992).

Author Photo by Mike Wilkshire

LARRY MATHEWS teaches in the English department at Memorial University of Newfoundland. His short fiction has appeared in a number of journals and anthologies, and in his collection of stories *The Sandblasting Hall of Fame* (2003). *The Artificial Newfoundlander* is his first novel. He lives in St. John's with the writer Claire Wilkshire and their children, Timothy and Sally.